D1188508

THE BOBBSEY TWINS IN THE LAND OF COTTON

"A prize to the one who picks the most!"

THE BOBBSEY TWINS IN THE LAND OF COTTON

By LAURA LEE HOPE

GROSSET & DUNLAP
PUBLISHERS NEW YORK

PRINTED IN THE UNITED STATES OF AMERICA

The Bobbsey Twins in the Land of Cotton

CONTENTS

CHAPTER I

A VISITOR

"HERE it goes!" cried Freddie Bobbsey as he sped down a grassy field.

Behind the small boy was a big red kite. It fluttered and dipped. Then the wind caught it. Freddie tugged at the spool of cord in his hand, but something went wrong. The kite dropped to the ground, dragged along the earth for a few feet, then stopped.

"I thought I had it going that time," said the lad, disappointed.

"You should have let out the string as soon as the kite caught the wind," replied his brother Bert, who was a few years older. "Here, I'll show you how."

He took the spool from Freddie's hand and set off at a run down the field. This time the kite stayed up and soon was flying skyward.

"I can do it now, Bert. Please!" Freddie panted, catching up to the bigger boy.

He took the spool, and both boys watched the red kite as it soared higher and higher.

"Here come Flossie and Nan," said Freddie

after a moment. "I suppose they'll want us to play something, but I'd rather fly my kite."

As their twin sisters came closer, the boys could see that Flossie carried a prettily dressed rag doll. She was holding it tightly in her arms. Nan had a slip of paper which she waved at them excitedly.

"It's a telegram from Susan Percy," she called. "It says she'll be here late this afternoon. Won't it be fun, meeting a grown-up cousin we don't even remember? I wonder what she will be like."

"Dinah says she's from the Land of Cotton," said Flossie, and added, "Just like my dolly."

Alas for Flossie! As she held up her beloved rag baby, a shaggy, yellow dog dashed past. With a yelp the animal grabbed the doll in its teeth and ran off into some bushes!

Nan and Bert gave chase but they were no match for the small dog. He dodged and twisted in and out among the bushes. Finally he disappeared altogether in a thicket of vines and tall grasses.

"Poor Flossie!" said Nan. "She loved that doll. It was sent to her from the Land of Cotton by Susan Percy. I don't want to tell our cousin it's gone."

"It's a shame!" agreed Bert.

Scratched and panting, he and Nan returned to the field where they found Freddie in tears.

"Bad Danny Rugg came," he cried, "and took my kite!"

Now Danny Rugg, a boy a little older than Bert, was a bully who never missed a chance to play a mean trick. He had grabbed the spool of cord from Freddie and run away when the kite caught in a tree.

Bert climbed the tree and got Freddie's toy, but the bright-colored kite was ruined!

"I held on to the cord and yelled," Freddie explained, "but Danny was too strong for me."

"Never mind, Daddy will get you

another kite," said Bert. "I'll settle with Danny!"

When they reached home a few minutes later, dear old Dinah, the Negro cook, opened the door. "Your cousin from the Land of Cotton is here." She beamed. "She's in the living room with your mother."

"Oh, Dinah, you mean Susan Percy? How wonderful!" cried Nan.

She started eagerly toward the other room, then stopped suddenly. Being a motherly little person, she remembered how dirty all the Bobbsey children were after their play in the fields. She shooed them upstairs to wash and comb their hair before meeting Susan Percy.

"What do you s'pose she'll be like, Nan?" asked Flossie, drawing back as her big sister ran a comb through her tangled curls.

"Oh, like us, I guess, only prettier. It must be lovely to live down South," said Nan, as she straightened the bow at the back of Flossie's pink dress. "I'd like to go there sometime."

"Well, maybe we can. Dinah says if you only think about a thing hard enough, 'most anything can happen," said Flossie.

At last the little twins, after much fussing, were neat and ready to go downstairs. Then Nan found that Bert was not around.

"I think he went to find Danny Rugg. Maybe he'll make him give me a new kite," Freddie explained.

"We'll go downstairs, anyway. And please, Freddie and Flossie, don't talk too much and don't get into any mischief," begged Nan.

The little twins promised to be good. In another moment they were standing in the doorway of the living room, waiting to greet Susan.

Susan Percy was indeed a very pretty young lady and a very friendly one, too. She went over to Nan at once and kissed her warmly. Then she hugged the little twins and drew them all into the room.

"Well, I declare, Nan has grown so much I wouldn't have known her," she said. "And the last time I saw you, Freddie and Flossie, you were in two tiny cribs, the cutest little babies I had ever seen. And you looked exactly alike."

"We're big now," said Freddie, who didn't like being called a "cute little baby."

"Yes, indeed, and I'm sure you are quite the man of the family," Susan smiled, and glanced about her. "Isn't there another twin, though? I'm sure I remember four of you."

"The other is Bert, Nan's twin," explained Mrs. Bobbsey.

She had been sitting in one corner of the couch, quietly enjoying the meeting of the cousins. Now she asked Freddie and Flossie to sit down beside her, and smiled at Susan.

"Suppose you go on with what you were telling me when the children came in," she suggested. "They will be interested in your plans too, I know."

"Oh, yes, please tell us," urged Nan, drawing a chair as close as she could to the visitor. "Mother said you are going to be a bridesmaid at someone's wedding."

"Yes, my school chum is to be married and I'm to be there. We made a pledge long ago to be at each other's weddings. It's very nice of you to let me visit you on my way to her home."

"It will be *fun* having you," said Nan eagerly.

"And you can tell us all about the Land of Cotton," Flossie chimed in.

"But not just now," smiled Flossie's mother. "Just before you children came in," she added, "Susan was saying something about a mysterious disappearance at her house. Some valuable silver pieces and vases were taken. Wasn't that it, Susan, and your family hasn't been able to find them?"

"Yes. It's all very strange. Mother feels bad because the things that were stolen have been in the family for such a long time," said the visitor, her face clouding. "The one she loved most belonged to my great-aunt Susan. It's almost exactly like the one you have there."

She nodded toward a black and gold vase standing on the mantel above the fireplace.

"Perhaps this is the mate to the one your mother had. It has been in our family a long time," said Mrs. Bobbsey. "If you like, you may have this one. Give it to your mother for her birthday from me."

Susan was about to say something in reply, when Freddie jumped up on the arm of the couch and reached for the beautiful vase.

"That's my bank!" he cried. "I have to get my money—"

Suddenly everyone gasped! The vase slipped from Freddie's hand and crashed to the floor!

CHAPTER II

A MEAN BOY

"OH, Freddie, look what you have done!" cried Mrs. Bobbsey.

The little boy got down on his knees and began to pick up the pieces of the broken vase. As usual, he was very sorry for his carelessness. He held up a few pennies which were scattered on the floor.

"These are my savings," he said. "Maybe they will pay to have the vase fixed. I'm awfully sorry I dropped it, Mother."

Mrs. Bobbsey accepted the pennies. She knew they would not go very far toward having the vase mended, but she felt it might teach Freddie to be more careful the next time.

"It isn't broken badly," said Nan, who had been examining the pieces. "I think it can be put together so the places won't show. Shall I take the vase to the shop tomorrow, Mother?"

Mrs. Bobbsey said that would be very helpful, so Nan put the pieces in a bag. Freddie was sent upstairs to think things over. When it was quiet again, Flossie begged to be told more about the

Land of Cotton and the plantation called Great Oaks where Susan Percy lived.

"You have lots and lots of cotton, haven't you?" the little girl asked.

"Well, most everybody grows it," her cousin answered. "We do on our plantation. In fact," she added with a smile, "I was Queen of the Cotton Ball last year."

Flossie clapped her hands delightedly. "We know all about queens, don't we, Nan?" she laughed. "Cousin Susan should have seen the one we had at the Ice Carnival last winter."

Susan asked about the Ice Carnival, and her question brought out the story of a great many happenings in the lives of the Bobbsey Twins. She learned a good deal about her young cousins and the life they lived in Lakeport with Mother and Daddy Bobbsey.

They told her stories about Dinah, the cook, and her husband Sam, who drove the car and was general handy man about the place. Susan heard about their two dogs; Snap, who was older and gentle, and young Waggo, the fox terrier, who was always getting into mischief.

Last and perhaps best of all, the twins told of their recent adventures at the Ice Carnival. Susan declared she could almost see beautiful Fairy Lake and the Ice Palace all a-glimmer under the lights.

"You must have had a wonderful time. I can almost feel the snowflakes on my face!" she laughed.

"You must have had fun at the Cotton Ball. It sounds lovely. Won't you tell us about it?" begged Nan.

"Have you a really big plantation? And do you ride horses all day long?" Flossie wanted to know.

"Well, not quite all day long," laughed Susan, "though we do ride a great deal. You would like it down there."

Flossie now told of how the bad dog had taken the lovely rag doll Susan Percy had sent to her. At once her grown-up cousin said she would see to it that the little girl would receive another one very soon.

At this point Bert came home from a search for Danny Rugg. He had not found the bully. He was greeted joyfully by Flossie, and led into the family circle.

"This is Susan Percy. Isn't she pretty? And she lives at a lovely place called Great Oaks in the Land of Cotton."

Bert liked his attractive, dark-haired cousin at once. Soon he was listening as eagerly as the others to her stories of plantation life.

"But we have been having trouble lately," said Susan, frowning.

"You mean about the robbery?" asked Nan.

"Yes, if you can call it that. Mother always speaks of it as 'the mysterious disappearance.' You see, she won't believe that anyone on the plantation would steal our fine old silver candlesticks and bowls and plates."

"And still one of them might have been the thief," Bert suggested.

"We don't think so," said Susan, leaning forward earnestly, "but we felt that we should notify the sheriff."

"And nothing was discovered?" asked Mrs. Bobbsey.

"Not a thing. The police searched everywhere—the house, the cabins, and the barns—in fact, all the buildings on the plantation. So Mother decided," said Susan, settling back with a little smile, "that she had been right. The servants were innocent, and never should have been questioned in the first place."

"It's very strange," said Mrs. Bobbsey.

"But someone must have stolen the things," said Flossie, wide-eyed. "They couldn't just get up and walk off by themselves."

"That's it, you see. That's the mystery," Susan pointed out. "If no one from the plantation took them, then someone from the outside must have been the thief."

"That's possible, isn't it?" asked Nan.

"Yes, but there is another point," continued Cousin Susan. "If a stranger had set foot in our house—or on the grounds anywhere near the house, for that matter—our hunting dogs would have set up a terrific howling."

"And they didn't?" asked Bert.

"No. There was no disturbance at all," Susan replied. "If the servants are innocent, and no stranger came near the place, then where did our good silver and other heirlooms disappear? They are gone—that much we do know."

"It *is* strange that the dogs were quiet if there was a thief about," said Mrs. Bobbsey.

"Perhaps they are old, and were tired like our dog Snap," Flossie suggested, "and just couldn't be bothered to make a fuss."

"No, ours are hunting dogs and they are trained to make a fuss. They tell us when strangers are about," explained Susan.

"It is almost like a mystery in a story book," said Nan thoughtfully.

"We could solve it, though. Anyway, Freddie could. He's a fine detective," Flossie boasted.

Now Freddie was very young, but already there were many things he wanted to be. One was to become a fireman and put out big blazes. Another was to be a detective and help the police.

"If you could find out what has become of our missing heirlooms we would be very happy," Susan said with a smile. "Why don't you all come down to visit us, anyway?"

"Oh, I wish we could," the twins said together.

Everybody in the Bobbsey family loved Susan Percy. Even sleepy Snap consented to stay awake long enough to put a heavy paw in her hand and permit himself to be scratched behind the ear.

And as for Waggo! After dinner he went through all his tricks twice over. He played dead, shook hands, and fetched all sorts of articles for his young masters. Finally he jumped right into Susan's lap and licked her face with such friendliness that Bert had to come to the rescue!

"I declare, I never saw a smarter dog," Susan laughed.

"I guess there never was a smarter dog in all the world," agreed Freddie, hugging Waggo to him.

The next morning Bert left the house early. He was determined to find Danny Rugg this time and settle with him about the ruined kite.

The meeting was not to take place the way he had wished, however. The Bobbsey boy took a short cut across a path that led to Danny's house. As he was passing a tree near the Ruggs' garden, something came from behind the trunk and struck him a hard blow in the face.

Taken by surprise, Bert staggered backward. He caught his foot in a root and fell to the ground. The breath was knocked from him for several seconds, and he could not stir. When he finally got to a sitting position, he caught sight of Danny running up the street.

"Come back here!" shouted Bert, but the fleeing boy paid no attention.

Bert could understand the whole thing now. Danny must have seen him coming. Feeling that the Bobbsey boy might try to fight with him over the kite, he had decided to get in the first blow.

"So he hid behind the tree and hit me before I could see what was coming. That's a fine way to fight, that is!" said Bert in scorn.

The lad's first impulse was to go after Danny and teach him a lesson he would never forget.

But second thought told him that the bully would take good care to keep out of sight, at least that day. In disgust, Bert turned his steps toward home, holding a hand over his swollen eye.

He had hoped to be able to reach his room

without being noticed. But Flossie spied him and cried: "Ooh, Bert has a black eye!"

There was nothing to do then but tell the whole story. The other twins felt very sorry for the boy. Dinah went to get a bit of raw beefsteak, which she said would keep the swelling down.

It was Mr. Bobbsey who did the most to cheer Bert, however. Coming home in the afternoon, he suggested that the whole family go to Willow Reservoir for a picnic supper.

"I feel better already." Bert grinned as everyone pitched in to pack some food.

Soon they were riding along in the car. They came to a lovely park across the road from the reservoir, and Mr. Bobbsey turned in. The children saw many long tables with benches where people might eat their picnic lunches.

"There are fireplaces to cook our hamburgers," said Nan.

"This is going to be a special kind of supper," said the twins' father, "a sort of party to say good-bye. I have to take a trip—a business trip down South."

"Oh, Daddy, how wonderful!" cried Flossie. "Are you going to the Land of Cotton?"

"Couldn't we go with you?" asked Nan and Bert together.

"Oh, yes, Daddy, please take us!" added Freddie.

"Not another word will I say until supper is on the table," said Daddy Bobbsey with a smile.

CHAPTER III

THE PICNIC

EAGER to hear what Daddy Bobbsey would say, the children hurried about to get the picnic supper ready. Bert found wood and built a fire. His father cooked the hamburgers.

"I'm hungry enough to eat the side of a barn!" he said with a twinkle in his eye.

Although the thought of their father trying to eat the side of a barn made the little twins laugh, they agreed that they were pretty hungry, too. They helped to get things ready by unpacking the paper napkins and cups. Nan and Susan spread the tablecloth, then Mother Bobbsey put out the knives, forks, spoons and paper plates.

Soon the fragrance of frying meat told them the meal was ready, so everyone sat down. Two little squirrels came to join them, and a bird in a near-by tree sang for them while they were eating.

"Now tell us about this southern trip," Mrs. Bobbsey begged her husband. "Will you go this month?"

"Yes, I must. It's because of the special work I'm doing on the old Washington Hotel. I am to sell them all the lumber they need to fix it up."

"You have piles and piles of boards at your lumber yard," said Freddie.

"Yes, Little Fireman, I have," replied Daddy Bobbsey, "but no boards old enough and beautiful enough to match the ones in the hotel. That was built over a hundred years ago, you see."

"Do they have old boards in the Land of Cotton, Daddy?" asked Flossie.

"Yes, Fat Fairy," replied her father.

"Couldn't you take us with you, Dad?" asked Bert, adding eagerly, "It would be a swell trip."

Mr. Bobbsey shook his head. "I've been trying to think how I could manage to take you all along," he confessed. "But I'm afraid it can't be done. The car will be crowded with luggage and samples of lumber. There won't be any room for the family at all. I'm sorry, but that's the way it is."

"Dinah says if you wish for something hard enough, maybe you will get it," said Flossie. "I'm going to wish and wish."

With that she closed her eyes tightly, making her face screw up into such a little ball that everyone had to laugh.

After supper the twins played "Indians and Settlers," and Freddie had a grand time practicing a war whoop. Once he went after Flossie and chased her, screaming happily, across the road. Without thinking, the little girl ran out on a platform which was over the water in the big reservoir. As her brother followed, Flossie turned to keep him off and stumbled.

Plop!

She hit the water with a loud splash! Then Freddie stopped being an Indian. Now he was only a very frightened little boy, shouting for help.

"Flossie's drowning! Help! He-elp!" he yelled. "Somebody come!"

In two seconds Bert and Nan reached the platform. They found their little sister struggling and kicking in the water only a few feet below them. Quickly, Bert let down a rope which he had been using in the game to bind Nan to a tree. Flossie seized it, and in another moment was back on the platform, a very wet child.

"I wasn't going to drown." She frowned at Freddie, as the water ran off her. "You know I can swim."

"Yes, but you shouldn't have been swimming," teased Bert. "Can't you see that sign over there?"

He pointed to large, black words reading:

"THIS IS DRINKING WATER.
DO NOT SWIM IN IT!"

They all laughed and said they guessed nobody would notice any difference in the water! A few moments later Flossie was wrapped in a steamer robe. Her little cotton dress was hung from the branch of a tree, while she sat before the fire and listened to Susan Percy tell stories of the Southland. Then the young woman said she must leave the next day.

"You have been so kind to me, I'll never forget it," she added in her soft voice. "And don't forget that Mother and Dad and I will be expecting you at Great Oaks for a visit some time."

The following morning the train whisked the twins' cousin away on her journey to New York, where she was to be a bridesmaid at the wedding of her school chum. For a while they missed her. Then Bert read an item in the newspaper which made them forget her for the time being.

"There's going to be a pet show in Hilltown," he said. "Wouldn't it be fun to enter Waggo? He has lots of good points and he's smart. I bet he'd get a prize."

"It *would* be fun," replied Nan. "Let's do it, Bert. We can start training him right away for the show!"

"Good idea," agreed her twin.

Dinah, who was in the room, flicked her duster over a tabletop and said gloomily, "If it's Waggo you're talking about, you'll have to find him first!"

"Find him," repeated Nan, staring at Dinah. "Why, he's in his kennel this very minute."

The cook shook her head dolefully. "He hasn't been back since last night."

The twins gave Dinah a startled glance, then ran to the back yard to see for themselves. Sure enough, there was no sign of Waggo there.

Alarmed, the twins searched for a clue to the dog's disappearance. Suddenly Nan cried, "Look!" and pointed to a paper tacked to the kennel wall. Over her shoulder the children saw a strange message.

CHAPTER IV

THE SEARCH FOR WAGGO

"WHAT does it say?" asked Freddie.

Slowly Bert read the words, tracing them out with his finger. " 'I kidnaped your dog. If you want him, put $5 in the oak tree by your house.' "

"Wh-what does that mean?" asked Flossie, big-eyed.

"I'm afraid it means someone has stolen our Waggo," said Nan, putting an arm about the little girl, "and wants us to pay five dollars to get him back."

"Of all the mean tricks!" said Bert, crumpling the paper in his hand.

Flossie began to cry, and Freddie's lip quivered, as if he were not very far from tears himself.

"What are we going to do now?" he demanded.

That was a question no one seemed to know how to answer. Several plans were suggested by the anxious children. It was finally decided to wait until Daddy and Mother Bobbsey should come home, and then ask them.

In the meantime the twins started a search. They went to the houses of all their playmates, and Freddie tired out poor Snap taking him through the woods and fields around the Bobbsey house. But all with no result.

"Maybe we should put the money in the oak tree the way the note said," Flossie suggested. "Then when the thief comes to get the five dollars, we can catch him."

"And sit up all night to do it, I suppose!" said Bert.

Nevertheless, the more they thought of it, the more sensible Flossie's idea seemed. So the three children put all their savings together—Freddie's had been given to mend the vase. By counting their nickels and dimes and pennies, they had just five dollars and six cents.

The money was enclosed in one of Mother Bobbsey's large envelopes. With a good deal of advice from the others, Bert climbed the oak tree at the side of their house. He fastened the envelope to a branch not too far from the ground, yet far enough so that the money would not be seen and taken by some passer-by.

When Mr. Bobbsey reached home he felt they should notify the police. This the children did not want him to do. They were afraid that the wicked person who had stolen Waggo would injure their pet if the police were put on his trail.

"All right," he agreed. "I'll wait until tomorrow."

When darkness came and still there was no

sign of Waggo or his kidnaper, the Bobbseys felt very sad indeed. Many times during dinner, one or another of them would jump up and run to the door, expecting to hear a bark or a familiar scratching sound.

"I didn't know there was anyone so mean in this whole world," said Flossie.

Even Snap was restless. When told to lie down, he always obeyed, but was up again the next instant to prowl about and sniff at the doors and windows.

Once during the night Bert thought he heard Waggo bark. He rushed downstairs, expecting to find his pet, but outside the door everything was silent and dark.

In the morning the first thing the twins did was run to the oak tree to see if the envelope with their five dollars was still there. It was! No one had come to disturb it all night long.

"I wish we had a new idea," sighed Nan hopelessly.

"Suppose you go downtown and see about having the vase mended," suggested Mother Bobbsey. "You can ask about Waggo on the way. Someone may have seen him or can tell you where to look for him."

Although the twins asked over and over again on their way into the center of Lakeport, no one could give them news of their pet. But when they reached the shop where the vase was to be left, they turned up a clue.

Mr. Rand, the owner, examined the broken

pieces of the heirloom and said he could fix it so that no one would ever know it had been broken. Then he began to talk about his shop. He pointed to several fancy dog collars hanging on the wall.

"Most folks keep dogs, so I thought I'd sell things for their pets. I have leashes, collars, baskets and blankets. A man came in here just a little while ago," he added, leaning against the counter. "He bought a lot of things for his new dog. Smart animal it was, too. He could do a lot of tricks—shake hands and beg, roll over and play dead—"

"Mr. Rand, do you know where that man lives?" Nan broke in excitedly.

"Why, yes, I do. I'm to send the things over to him. Why do you want to know?"

"It's a clue," Freddie all but shouted.

"Please give us the address, Mr. Rand," begged Bert.

"We just have to see that dog!" added Flossie.

Because the man knew the Bobbsey Twins so well, he scribbled the address on a slip of paper and handed it to Nan.

The children thanked the shopkeeper and hurried off to the street indicated on the slip of paper.

"Do you think it—really—is—Waggo?" panted Flossie, skipping and running along in an effort to keep up with Nan and Bert.

"We'll soon know," said her brother, as they turned a corner. "This is the street. The house ought to be right along here somewhere."

When they reached the correct number, the children halted uncertainly. This house did not look like one a person who would kidnap little dogs to get money would live in! It was large and newly painted white. It was set well back from the street and had a lovely flower garden in front of it.

A big collie on the porch pricked up his ears as the children started rather slowly up the walk. The animal rose to his feet and growled softly, deep down in his throat.

"I—I don't think he likes us very much," said Flossie, reaching for Nan's hand.

At this moment the front door opened. A well-dressed, pleasant-faced man came out on the porch. He spoke gently to the dog and smiled at the children.

"Lie down, Major!" he said to the animal, and to the twins he added, "He won't hurt you, now that he knows you're friends. Won't you come in?"

"Is that—is that the only dog you have?" Freddie blurted out.

"Why, yes. Should I have another?" asked the collie's owner, his eyes twinkling.

Bert decided that it was time to explain why they were there. He told frankly, in as few words as possible, about Waggo's disappearance, the note and the oak tree. He ended with the "clue" they had got at Mr. Rand's shop; that this man's dog was a new one and could do tricks.

"So you thought I had your Waggo," the collie's master said thoughtfully.

"I'm afraid we've made a very stupid mistake, sir," Bert apologized. "I hope you will excuse us."

The man smiled. "I'm sorry I haven't been of any help to you. I'll keep my eyes open for your lost pet, though, and let you know if I hear anything."

The twins thanked him. Then they said a final word to the collie—who was now as friendly as you please—and turned homeward.

"Oh, look what's in front of our house!" cried Freddie as they entered their own street.

A large automobile and a trailer were parked before the Bobbsey home. Coming closer, the children saw that the trailer had a flat tire. The owner was busily unhooking one car from the other.

"May I help you?" Bert asked him.

"No!" the man answered unpleasantly.

"Your trailer has Southern license plates," said Nan. "Do you live—"

The owner did not wait to hear her question. He got into his automobile quickly and drove away, leaving the trailer standing there. The policeman on the beat strolled up a few minutes later and looked at the clumsy vehicle.

"Now I wonder where that came from. It isn't yours by any chance?" he asked the twins with a smile.

"Oh, don't I wish it was," sighed Flossie. "If

we had it, then Daddy could take us with him on his trip to the Land of Cotton!"

The trailer stayed in front of the house all day. Just after supper another policeman came to look at it; then he rang the Bobbsey doorbell.

"I believe your children saw the man who left this trailer here," he said to the twins' father. "We have just learned that it was stolen. I wonder if your boys and girls can tell me what the thief looks like."

Of course the children were very excited to hear this news. They all talked at once, trying to give a description of the unpleasant man who had left the trailer standing outside their house.

The big surprise came the next day. Mr. Bobbsey was called to the police station, where the sergeant behind the desk said to him:

"Your little girl told one of our men you are making a trip South. Now we wonder just where you are going, and if by any chance you can take the trailer with you. Mr. Hopper, the owner, lives in Flagville, and he is very eager to have his property back. Will your business take you near there?"

"Yes, it will," replied Mr. Bobbsey. "I'll think the matter over and let you know tomorrow."

On the way home he kept smiling to himself. Should he do it?

"The trailer is just what I need to take the whole family with me to the Land of Cotton," he thought.

CHAPTER V

A LOST LETTER

BY the time Mr. Bobbsey got home, the twins were in bed, but in the morning they heard the news that they could go with him. And were they excited!

"I'll put our luggage and the samples of lumber in the trailer," their daddy said. "Then the six of us can ride in the automobile."

Mother Bobbsey felt they should visit the Percys at the Great Oaks plantation, if it were convenient for her relatives to have them.

"I'll send a letter at once by air mail to Cousin Martha," she smiled. "You remember, she's Susan's mother," she told the twins.

"Please let me mail it," begged Flossie.

Her mother thought Daddy Bobbsey should take it to the post office at once, so he drove the little girl there in his car to post it. She ran into the building alone and found the right slot for the envelope.

But alas, the letter was never to get to Cousin Martha! Flossie was not very tall. When she reached up to the opening, she thought the envelope went through it. Instead it dropped outside, right into a big wastepaper basket which stood there. Happily Flossie went back to the car. After a while the janitor of the post office emptied the trash into the furnace!

Not knowing this, the Bobbseys waited eagerly for an answer. The twins talked and talked about what they were going to do at the Great Oaks plantation.

"Why don't you come with us, Dinah?" Flossie asked as she ran about the kitchen helping to make some cookies. "You and Sam used to live in the Land of Cotton. Wouldn't you like to go back there?"

"I sure would, honey," said Dinah, putting the cooky tin down on the kitchen table. "My uncle Eben's house is right near Colonel Percy's place."

"Wouldn't you like to go with us?" Flossie insisted.

"What I want isn't always what I get," said Dinah cheerfully. "Your daddy's shorthanded and needs Sam at the lumber yard. Besides, I reckon I ought to be here when little old Waggo comes home."

"Let's hope Waggo will be here by the time we get back from our trip," said the twins' mother. "Now we must think about what clothes to take along."

Nan and Flossie helped Mrs. Bobbsey with this, but Freddie was not interested. He was eager to do his part, though, so he took out the garden hose and started to wash the trailer.

"I'll make our house on wheels real clean," he said to himself.

Happily Freddie played the hose over the trailer, up and down and from side to side. Everything might have been all right if the little boy had remembered to close the door and windows. But he forgot to do so! The inside, as well as the outside of the trailer, got a bath.

"Oh, Freddie, Freddie!" cried Mrs. Bobbsey

when she saw the wet, messy interior. "You will have to mop up that water right away and take every cushion outside."

The little boy set to work, but his mother and Dinah had to help him. Fortunately, by the time Daddy Bobbsey reached home, the trailer was dry and in good condition again.

The twins' father laughed when they all rushed out to meet him to hear his plans for the trip. He teased them a little at first. Then he said that he had made all arrangements. They could start as soon as they should hear from Cousin Martha Percy.

Everyone was merry at dinner except Bert. He seemed rather glum and out of sorts. When Nan asked him about this, he told her he had begun to suspect Danny Rugg of having stolen Waggo. But he had learned the boy had gone away to visit an uncle, so he guessed he was wrong.

"Somebody should be here to see that Waggo practices his tricks in case he should come back," Bert added. "And who will enter him in the show if I'm not at home? Perhaps I shouldn't go down South."

"I can tend to that all right, Bert," said Dinah, putting a plate of hot muffins on the table.

"But I ought to earn the money for the fee. I haven't any now that—" Bert broke off and stared at his brothers and sisters. "That reminds me! Has anyone looked to see if the money we put in the tree is gone?"

No one had, of course. They had been too excited about the trip to think of looking for the envelope!

Impatiently they waited for Dinah to bring in the dessert. As soon as the meal was over, they excused themselves and ran out into the garden.

The envelope was gone!

"Does that mean the kidnaper has been here?" asked Nan in a hushed voice.

"And we never saw him, and Snap never barked, or anything!" said Freddie.

"No, and the kidnaper hasn't brought back Waggo, either," said Bert slowly. "He took the money all right, but Waggo's still missing."

The children would not give up hope of Waggo's safe return. Bert went ahead with his plans to enter the little dog in the show. Mr. Bobbsey even suggested a way for the lad to earn the entry fee.

"I'm shorthanded at the yard," the boy's father said. "How about helping me out? Two days' pay should take care of entering Waggo in the show."

So Bert went to the lumber yard with Daddy Bobbsey. At home all was bustle and excitement as Mrs. Bobbsey got things ready for the trip. She thought it strange that no answer to her letter had come from Cousin Martha Percy at Great Oaks.

"I can't understand it," she told herself.

The next day Flossie decided to do something about this. When luncheon was ready, she was nowhere about. Nan and Freddie searched everywhere but could not find their little sister.

Nan remembered that Flossie had gone up to the attic. So they went to the top floor to search among the luggage, old pieces of furniture and discarded toys. It was possible the little girl had fallen asleep there.

"Maybe she's in one of the trunks," Freddie suggested when they did not find her.

This did not seem very likely, but Mrs. Bobbsey knew it was wise to look everywhere. So they opened all the trunks, including the one that was full to the top with pieces of silk and ribbon.

"This is serious," said Mrs. Bobbsey. "I believe I'd better telephone to Daddy. He can take the car and hunt for Flossie."

After this was done, Nan began to call up her friends in the hope that one of them might have seen her little sister. At last her efforts were rewarded. Nellie Parks reported that Flossie had passed her house about an hour before. She had turned down the street toward the post office.

"I'll run over there," offered Nan, dashing from the house.

She found the little girl talking with the friendly postmaster, who was going through the early afternoon mail to see if there was a letter for the Bobbseys from Cousin Martha Percy!

"I just couldn't wait another minute," said Flossie.

There was no letter from Great Oaks plantation. Mrs. Bobbsey was disappointed, for she felt that a trip to the Land of Cotton would not be so pleasant if they should have to stay in a hotel at the end of their journey.

Bert could not sleep well that night, for he kept thinking about Waggo. Early the next morning before anyone was downstairs, he thought he heard a bark. Quickly he put on bathrobe and slippers and went to look outside.

He saw nothing unusual. A glance at Waggo's kennel told him it still was empty. He decided to look in the trailer which had been put in the Bobbseys' back yard. Opening the door to it, he gasped.

Curled up on the floor was a boy about Bert's own age! Under his head was a ragged coat being used for a pillow. An old rug was drawn over him for warmth. The lad was fast asleep!

CHAPTER VI

TINKY

BERT must have made some noise; or perhaps it was the faint squeak of the trailer door. Anyway, some sound roused the sleeper. The strange boy sat up with a start, and stared at Bert with frightened eyes.

"I ain't hurt you none. You ain't got no call to worry me," he said defiantly.

"I was looking for my lost dog Waggo," explained the Bobbsey boy.

"He ain't in here with me," replied the lad.

"Why are *you* here?" Bert asked curiously.

"I was only restin', that's what, before you come and roused me up. A feller has a right to sleep, I guess, and—and the ground's kind of cold, so I crept in here."

"Sure, I know," said Bert, beginning to be sorry for the poor, shivering boy. "What is your name?"

"They call me Tinky," he responded quietly.

"Haven't you any home?" asked Bert in surprise.

"I have a home, all right, but it ain't around

here. And I don't have to answer none of your questions neither," he grumbled.

"Well, you needn't act like this. I was just going to help you, that's all," said Bert kindly. He hesitated. Then, as he heard Dinah rattling pots and pans in the kitchen, he added, "It's almost time to eat. How about having some breakfast with us?"

The boy's eyes filled with tears, but he brushed a hand across them.

"I ain't hungry," he muttered. "You ain't got no call to feed me, anyway."

"Maybe not, but you'll be glad I did, once you get a taste of Dinah's cooking," said Bert cheerfully.

A delicious odor of frying bacon came from the kitchen, across the garden and in through the door of the trailer. The strange boy sniffed—and smiled.

"I guess I could do with a little corn pone," he said.

"Well, I don't know about that," replied Bert. "But I can promise some pretty swell bacon and eggs. Come along."

"You sure this ain't no trick?" the boy asked. "You ain't goin' to have me arrested, or nothin' like that?"

"Say, do I look like the kind of guy who would do that?" Bert asked.

He stood still, so that the other lad could get a good look at him. After a few seconds the boy nodded as if satisfied.

"No, I guess you don't," he said, and followed his new friend into the house.

Bert managed to get the stranger upstairs without anyone seeing him. He gave him a clean towel and face cloth, a brush and comb. By the time the Bobbsey boy was dressed, his young guest had washed all the dirt from his face and hands. He had tried to slick back his wild, unruly hair.

"Come on, let's get something to eat," said Bert briskly.

Still the strange lad held back. "I ain't hardly fit to eat with decent folks," he said. "Reckon your ma and pa won't like the look of me."

It was Mrs. Bobbsey who settled the question. Hearing voices on the stairs, she came out to see who was there. On one step stood the shabbiest, most starved-looking lad she had ever seen!

"This is Tinky, Mother," said Bert quickly. "He doesn't live around here. He—"

Mother Bobbsey waited to hear no more. Without showing any surprise, she took the hungry lad by the hand and led him into the warm, sunny dining room.

"Bert has brought a little friend to breakfast," she said to Mr. Bobbsey, who was the only one at the table. "Isn't it nice that Dinah made more muffins than usual this morning? There will be plenty for all of us."

"Er—er—yes," said Mr. Bobbsey. "Yes, indeed. Of course! We are always glad to see

Bert's friends. Sit right down, my boy, and make yourself at home."

Shyly the lad accepted the chair Bert drew up for him and murmured, "Thank ye kindly."

Dinah brought in oatmeal and set a bowl of it at the visitor's place. He refused the pitcher of cream that Mr. Bobbsey pushed toward him and asked for butter instead.

"Don't you use cream on your cereal?" asked Bert.

"Reckon we're more used to butter and salt on porridge where I come from," replied the lad.

"I knew you were from the Land of Cotton," said Dinah, beaming at the young guest. "Never touched cream on porridge myself till I came up North. What part are you from, honey child?"

"No questions now, Dinah, please," warned Mrs. Bobbsey.

A few moments later she went upstairs and returned with Nan and the little twins. Bert guessed that his mother had told the children about their strange visitor and had warned them not to ask questions. The little twins were very good all during the meal.

"Do you like lots of butter on your muffin?" asked Freddie of their guest.

Before the stranger could reply, Flossie pointed out that most of Freddie's butter was around his mouth. Nan, too, tried her best to put Tinky at his ease. Soon the lad began to forget his shyness. Once or twice he even laughed at some funny remark of Bert's.

"Won't you tell us about the place where you live?" asked Mother Bobbsey after they had finished eating.

"Reckon Dinah knew what she was talkin' about when she said I'm from the Land of Cotton. I ain't never knowed nothin' all my life but cotton and lumber. I got purty sick of it, and so I made up my mind to run off.

"I'd had it in my mind a good long time," the lad continued, " 'cause I wanted to see the world. So I kep' some money by me that my pa had give me for work I did on the farm. Then one day I seed a funny-looking little house standin' in the road alongside our field. It was hooked up to the car."

"A trailer!" cried Bert. "Like the one I found you in this morning," he added when Tinky did not know what he meant.

"Go on," urged Daddy Bobbsey. "The trailer gave you an idea how you could run away from your mother and father. Is that it?"

The lad was silent for a moment or two, then answered, "I reckon so. I wanted to get a fine job up No'th. I thought it would be easy, once I got away from our county."

"What did you do then?" asked Bert.

"The man in the car went up to our house—to git some milk and eggs, I reckon. And while he was gone, I went up to the little house—the trailer—and tried the door. I found it opened easy. So I got inside and hid. When the man came back, he started off without ever knowin' I was inside."

"A trailer stowaway!" exclaimed Bert.

Tinky went on to tell of his adventures on the journey North. He had grown more and more lonesome. When they stopped at night, he would slip out and buy or beg a little food. Often he slept in an open field or a barn.

"The man stayed in the house—trailer—at night, you see, and I was skeered he'd catch me," Tinky explained.

"And so?" prompted Mother Bobbsey gently.

"There ain't much more to tell, ma'am. We kept going farther No'th and finally came here. Then I left the trailer and looked for work. But no one wanted to hire me, 'cause I was little and skinny, and my clothes was hardly decent."

"Then this trailer at our house is the same one you came up in!" said Nan.

"I reckon it is," replied the boy. "It was the only home I knew, so when I saw it again, I came back last night to sleep in it."

Mr. and Mrs. Bobbsey questioned the boy further, and found out where his father's farm was. They promised to let Tinky's people know he was alive and well, and would find some way to send him back South.

"That man stole the trailer," said Freddie. "We're going to take it back to the owner."

"You all are goin' to the Southland?" asked Tinky.

"Yes," replied Flossie excitedly. "Maybe we can take you home."

Mrs. Bobbsey interrupted to say that she wanted Tinky to take a bath and put on some of Bert's clothes. Later that day, after a trip to the barber shop for a haircut, the little guest, a good deal tidier than when Bert first had seen him, went with his new friend to Mr. Bobbsey's lumber yard.

The lad knew a great deal about the different kinds and grades of wood. Mr. Bobbsey was delighted and declared that perhaps Tinky might help him select lumber on their Southern trip.

"Perhaps I'll be able to get some from your father," he added, knowing that this would please the boy.

He was right. Tinky's face fairly glowed as he answered:

"Pa would sure admire to sell you some. There ain't no better lumberman around our parts than my pa!"

On their way home later that day, Bert told his new friend the story of their missing dog. He mentioned the note and the five dollars, which had been taken from the oak tree beside their house.

It was then that Tinky made an astonishing statement. "Reckon I know who took your money," he said.

CHAPTER VII

BERT'S DISCOVERY

"YOU know *what?*" Bert demanded, staring at Tinky.

The Bobbsey boy was astonished.

"Was the money in a big white envelope, and was it mostly in nickels and dimes with only a few twenty-five cent pieces?" Tinky asked.

"That's right. But how do you know?" Bert asked.

Tinky became sullen again as he answered, " 'Tweren't me took it, 'cause that's what you're thinkin'. 'Twas a man that was with me. He treated me better than a lot of folks, even if he was a tramp. He give me somethin' to eat, and he come along with me late yesterday afternoon when I was tryin' to find where the trailer was. He seed the envelope in the tree, so he climbed up and took it."

"What kind of a man was he? Did he have a little dog with him?" cried Bert in great excitement. "Try to think! It's important!"

Tinky could not tell very much about the tramp, except that he was a tall man with gray hair and—about this he was very sure—he had no dog with him.

"Let's find the man right away," urged Nan, when the rest of the Bobbsey family heard the story.

"We'll make him give Waggo back to us!" cried the little twins together.

Even Mr. Bobbsey thought the clue was worth following. Unwilling though Tinky was to tell more about the tramp who had been so kind to him, he did show Bert and his father the camp where the man lived with some other tramps.

There they found several ragged fellows grouped about a fire. Tinky looked at each one, then he reported that the man who had been his friend was not among them.

"Where'd Red go to?" the boy asked the tramps.

"He hopped a freight early this morning," replied one of them. "Don't know where he went."

"Did he have a dog with him?" Bert asked.

"Naw," another tramp answered.

"Reckon there never was no chance of Red's takin' Waggo," said Tinky. "He was mortal skeered of dogs. He told me so."

So that was that! Another clue had failed.

On the way home Mr. Bobbsey suggested that they stop at the police station. He was sure the officer there would like to ask Tinky some questions about the person who had stolen the trailer. He was right. The man in charge was very glad to see them.

"Did you notice any initials on the thief's traveling bags?" asked the sergeant who was sitting up high behind a desk.

"No, I didn't," replied Tinky. "And I never heerd him say a word, or get called by name."

"Can you think of anything special about him, or was there some article in his car or the trailer which would give us his name?" the smiling policeman questioned the boy.

After a few seconds the lad replied, "He had a big nose. One day he writ a letter and left it in the trailer. It said, 'Dear Joe,' and at the bottom it was signed 'Biff.' I reckon that's a very peculiar name, ain't it?"

"Yes, it is, son." The sergeant smiled. "Did you read what the letter said?"

"No, sir," Tinky answered. "The man writ the envelope later, and I never seed where it was goin' to."

As the boy could think of nothing else to tell about the thief, the officer thanked him, then said good-bye to the three callers.

"You have been a great help, Tinky," said the sergeant as they were going out the door.

When Mr. Bobbsey and the two boys reached the house, Nan and the little twins were disappointed to find that Waggo was not with them.

Flossie suggested putting another five dollars in the tree, but Mrs. Bobbsey would not allow this. Instead, Nan wrote a note begging for the return of their pet. She put it in the oak, and the twins felt better.

Dinah then said that she had decided to send her aunt Emma a radio if the Bobbseys would deliver it for her. Aunt Emma was the wife of Uncle Eben, whose farm was near Great Oaks plantation.

"I know they don't have a radio," said Dinah.

"Do they have electricity?" asked Bert quickly.

"Reckon not," replied Dinah.

"Then you'd better get a portable," advised the boy.

The cook thought Bert was very smart, and asked him to go with her to make the purchase. The other children begged to go along, so they all started out.

"Maybe we can get a good radio in a second-hand store," said Dinah.

Flossie and Freddie were delighted at this, because the place Nan suggested carried just about everything in the world. They were not much help when they arrived, for there was a lot to look at. Suddenly Flossie shrieked:

"Ooh, Indians!"

The little girl ran and hid behind Dinah.

"Indians!" Nan echoed. "Not in here, Flossie!"

"Oh, yes, there are," the little girl insisted, pointing to a dark corner of the store. "There's one right over there! And he has a big axe in his hand!"

The Indian proved to be a wooden one. The axe was wooden, too, and had a very dull edge.

"I was only playing," said Flossie, giggling, and promised to be quiet. "Where's Fred—oh!"

From another section of the store came a crash and a wail from her twin. The little boy

was found in a heap of toys of all sorts. They had fallen on him when he had tried to reach a model fire engine on a shelf above his head.

"Oh, dear!" cried Nan. Then as she saw that Freddie was all right, she added, "I hope nothing is broken."

Fortunately nothing was, and the toys were restored to their proper places. Nan took Freddie and Flossie firmly by their hands so they would not get into any more mischief.

Meanwhile Bert had been examining the radio Dinah liked best. He was very thorough. The shopkeeper was surprised that a boy of his age knew so much about batteries and wires and sound.

"I guess no dealer could put anything over on you," he said admiringly. "I believe you know more than I do!" he laughed.

When Bert approved of her choice, Dinah paid the man and proudly carried off her present for Aunt Emma. As soon as they reached home, Tinky became very interested in the little box.

"I reckon it's magic," he said.

He was a bit frightened when Bert turned one of the knobs and they heard a band playing Yankee Doodle! He wanted to know exactly how everything worked, so the Bobbsey boy said he would show him.

Bert opened the back of the box and put his hand inside to take out one of the tubes. Suddenly his fingers touched something that certainly did not belong in the works of any radio. He drew out the object and found that it was a small pocketbook, well-filled.

"Well, I never! A radio spoutin' money!" exclaimed Dinah, throwing up her hands.

"Better open the purse, Bert. It might have

the owner's address inside it," Nan suggested.

The pocketbook had several bills of small amount, and it contained a letter addressed to a Mrs. Anna Grayson at Forty-four Park Road, Lakeport.

"That's not far from here," said Bert. "This radio must have belonged to her."

"Let's go ask Mrs. Grayson if this is her property," Nan proposed.

"A radio is a funnier hiding place for money than a vase," said Freddie.

All the twins set off to find Forty-four Park Road. Tinky went to the lumber yard to help Mr. Bobbsey.

"Dad likes to have Tinky there. That boy sure knows a lot about lumber," said Bert.

"He doesn't know about a lot of other things like we do," said Freddie, trotting along sturdily to keep up with the older twins. "Did you see how scared he was when we first turned on the radio?"

"Yes, but afterward he thought it was wonderful," said Nan.

"He never saw a telephone before he came to our house, and he thought we ought to put wood in the gas stove to cook our supper," Flossie added.

"That's true," agreed Nan. "We Bobbseys are just lucky to live where we have those things. But Tinky's all right, so it just shows that a person doesn't need gas stoves and telephones to make him good."

By this time the children had reached Forty-four Park Road. They stopped before a small house which was badly in need of paint and repair. But the grass had been cut recently and a row of bright flowers bordered the walk.

"Whoever lives here must be rather poor," said Nan.

A small, gray-haired lady came to the door when they rang the bell. Her face looked tired and worried, but brightened at sight of the children. She asked in a soft voice what she could do for them.

"We have just found something and we think it belongs to you; that is, if you are Mrs. Anna Grayson," Nan said.

"Yes, that is my name. Please come inside," said the little lady. "I lost a purse some time ago," she added, when the children were grouped about her in her living room. "It had about twenty dollars in it, I think, in small bills and about a dollar more, perhaps, in change."

"It was a purse that we found!" cried Flossie, bouncing in delight on her chair.

The woman looked pleased. "I live alone and I am getting old and forgetful," she explained. "I have the habit of putting money in various places about the house. Sometimes I can't remember where I have hidden it."

"I do that, myself, lots of times," said Flossie, "not with money, but with other things."

Mrs. Grayson smiled and put her hand gently on the little girl's pretty curls. She leaned forward eagerly, as Bert took the purse from his pocket.

"Yes, that's it! And I think it has a letter inside it addressed to me. Oh, thank you a thousand times, my dears, for bringing this here. It means so much to me!"

When the children told where they had found the money, the woman recalled having put the pocketbook inside the radio.

"And I forgot to take it out before I sold the portable," she said.

She wanted to reward them, but the twins would not take anything.

"We're glad to do this," said Nan, smiling. "There *is* something you could do, though, that would be like a reward to us," she added.

The girl went on to tell about their missing dog and asked Mrs. Grayson to let them know if she should see Waggo.

"Waggo, did you say?" the woman inquired quickly. "I've heard that name recently. Let me see—" she paused. "Yes, I recall now."

The Bobbsey Twins held their breath, waiting for the answer.

"One night—not so long ago," Mrs. Grayson continued, "I went outside to call my cat in. Somebody came along the street, carrying a little dog. When it saw my cat, the dog tried to go after my pet."

"Did he?" asked Freddie, who had left his chair and was standing right in front of the speaker.

"No. The person held on tightly to the dog, I guess," the woman replied. "But I did hear him say, 'Stop that, Waggo! You behave yourself!' "

"What did this person look like?" questioned Bert quickly. "Was he old or young?"

"I really can't say," Mrs. Grayson answered. "It was so dark, I couldn't see very well. But I should guess it was either a boy or a man who is not very old."

In the talk that followed, the twins decided that Mrs. Grayson must have seen Waggo soon after he had been stolen. When they left her house, they tried to think how they could use this as a clue. Where had the thief gone? Who was he? Not one of the children could figure out a thing.

"Anyway, we know Waggo is alive," said Freddie. "And I hope he's getting enough to eat."

When the children neared their own home, they saw that someone in the uniform of a messenger boy was standing on their doorstep. Mother Bobbsey was just signing for a telegram.

"Maybe it's a message from the Land of Cotton!" Flossie cried. "Oh, I hope we're going to Great Oaks plantation!"

CHAPTER VIII

THE SECRET

IT DID not take the Bobbsey Twins long to reach their doorway after that! In just about a minute Mrs. Bobbsey was fairly overwhelmed by her children, who wanted to know if the telegram was from Cousin Martha Percy.

"Give me time to open it!" laughed their mother, as they crowded around her. "Yes, it is. And she wants us to visit her at Great Oaks—"

"Hooray!" shouted Freddie, turning a somersault.

"Gee, that's swell!" cried Bert.

He started to turn a handspring, remembered where he was in time, and hugged his mother instead.

"There's something strange about this message," Mrs. Bobbsey said after a moment. "It reads as if Cousin Martha had not received my air-mail letter. She says Susan wrote to her that we might come South and suggested an invitation to us to visit Great Oaks."

"Does it matter, Mother, so long as they want us to come?" asked Nan.

"No, I suppose not," said Mrs. Bobbsey, adding thoughtfully, "but I should like to know what happened to my letter!"

She never was to know; that matter was to remain a mystery to them always. The twins, their mother, and Dinah agreed that the invitation called for a special celebration. Oddly enough, it was not any one of them, but Sam, who suggested the best way to have one.

He had found out something which he whispered to Dinah. Dinah, in turn, told the secret to Mother Bobbsey, and she at once got in touch with Bert. The result was that the boy made a hurried trip downtown to make a purchase. Meanwhile the kitchen fairly hummed with activity, as the smiling cook worked on something special.

"Oh, happy day," she sang. "Oh, happy day—"

Just before dinner Mother Bobbsey told the secret to the younger twins. Flossie rushed upstairs to put on her best dress and comb her curly hair. Nan was too busy to help her, so the little girl got into all kinds of difficulties.

First, she couldn't make the buttons and buttonholes come out even. The comb became entangled in her hair, and poor Flossie pulled until the tears came. Her hair ribbon was tied a little crooked, and she put on two socks which did not match.

"Hello, everybody!" boomed a voice in the lower hall while this was going on.

Mr. Bobbsey was home! With him was Tinky. Learning of the telegram from Great Oaks, the twins' father said they would take Tinky to his home on their way South. This made the boy very happy.

Everyone was in gay spirits as Dinah announced that dinner was ready. She had prepared a real Southern meal, in honor of the little guest. And how Tinky enjoyed it—especially the freshly baked corn pone!

"Tastes just as good as Ma makes," he declared. "An' she's a pow'ful fine cook!"

When every plate was clean, Sam came in, bearing a huge bowl of ice cream. Dinah followed and, smiling broadly, held high a beautiful cake with lighted candles!

Immediately the twins burst into singing:

"Happy birthday to you,
Happy birthday to you,
Happy birthday, dear Tinky,
Happy birthday to you!"

As Dinah set the cake in front of the lad, his eyes filled with tears of joy. Shyly Tinky said, "I sure thank you all. I—I ain't never had a party."

Nan, touched, spoke up. "Now what you do is make a wish and try to blow out all the candles at once."

Tinky looked around. "I wish," he said, "that sometime I can do somethin' for the Bobbseys!"

Then he gave a mighty puff that would have blown out twice the number of candles on his cake, or so the twins said! The cake was one of the best Dinah ever had baked, and the vanilla ice cream was homemade, too. And were they delicious!

Just when Tinky was beginning to feel that nothing could make him any happier than he was at that minute, Bert appeared in the doorway with another surprise. He was carrying a large package wrapped in fancy paper and ribbon.

"To Tinky!" he said in a loud voice. "With best wishes for a happy birthday from *all* the Bobbsey family!"

He set the package down before the guest of honor. In wonder the little Southern boy looked from one to another, then down at the tissue-wrapped gift.

"Reckon I don't know what 'tis," he stammered.

"Open it and see," said Nan delightedly.

"It won't bite you," urged Freddie in excitement. "It's a present for you!"

Slowly Tinky pushed aside the paper covering. Before his eyes stood a small portable radio!

The boy was overjoyed. All he could do was stare at the handsome gift. He opened his mouth once or twice, but no words came out. He really was speechless!

He decided the Bobbseys must have read his thoughts. Ever since seeing the radio Dinah had bought, he had wanted one just like it to take home to his folks.

"Look, I'll show you how it works," said Bert. "It has a battery of its own, you see. You can use this radio anywhere—in the woods or in a car. We'll have some fun with it on our trip South."

"Oh, thank you, thank you," Tinky finally managed to say, as Bert was tuning in to the various stations. "I reckon I—"

He ceased speaking, for the Bobbsey Twins suddenly had stopped paying attention to him. They had heard a familiar bark.

Waggo was at the window!

The children were not mistaken. Though he vanished the next second, for just one breathless instant Waggo had been there!

Bert rushed to the window and flung up the screen. Nan and Freddie ran to the front door and out of the house.

"Here, Waggo, here, Waggo!" they cried happily.

But Waggo did not come. There was no answer to their eager calls, no sharp barking, no rush of a small dog glad to be home again. Flossie kept insisting:

"But I *saw* him. He was at the window, just as plain as could be. It *was* Waggo!"

"Maybe he got away from the one who stole him, but that person caught him again," said Nan.

Daddy Bobbsey got out the car and drove about the neighborhood, searching for the little dog. At home the twins called and called, and even used flashlights to peer into the dark fields.

They had no success at all. Waggo had left again, as mysteriously as before.

Freddie got up very early the next morning. He wanted to go down and look for footprints. "I'm the detective of the family," he said to himself.

Bert found him sometime later, examining

marks in the garden under a magnifying glass.

"Any luck?" asked the older boy.

"No. The steps are all mixed up," replied Freddie. "And I guess, anyway, most of the footprints belong to us," he added with a sigh.

His work was interrupted by the sound of the breakfast bell. It reminded him he had been up a long time! During the meal Mother Bobbsey told the children that she hoped they might start their trip South right after lunch.

"Your Daddy went to his office early to try to make arrangements," she told them.

Suitcases were packed carefully and these Bert and Sam put into the trailer. In the meantime Freddie and Flossie had gathered together their favorite toys. Along with a small fire engine and several dolls, there were boxes of games.

The children had been working for some time when Daddy Bobbsey came home. They thought he did not look very happy as he peered into the trailer.

I'm afraid you will have to take these things out again!" he said quietly.

The twins stared at their father in dismay. Did this mean they would have to give up the trip?

CHAPTER IX

CAMPING OUT

"YOU don't mean we aren't leaving after all, do you, Daddy?" asked Nan.

"Please don't make us stay home," begged Flossie.

"We were going to have such a lot of fun!" Freddie added.

Daddy Bobbsey looked surprised, then suddenly he smiled.

"I'm sorry if I upset you," he said. "We are going on the trip, of course. All I meant was that we can't take so many things in the trailer. It isn't coming back again, you know, but we and our baggage are. Had you forgotten?"

"Can't we take along any of our toys?" Flossie wanted to know.

"I'm afraid not, unless they are very little ones. Just one small doll," warned Daddy Bobbsey as he went off into the house.

The little twins took out the toys, and even Mother Bobbsey had to unpack a couple of suitcases! But the two portable radios stayed in, and so did the mended black and gold vase, which was to be a present to Cousin Martha Percy. The work on this had been done so well that it was almost impossible for anyone to tell where it had been broken. Freddie, who had caused the accident, felt mighty relieved.

When everything finally was ready, Sam and Dinah came to the door to see them off. The cook called last-minute messages to the family while they were getting settled in the car.

Nan sat in front with Mother and Daddy Bobbsey, while the little twins, Bert and Tinky, crowded into the back of the automobile.

"Good-bye, Sam! Good-bye, Dinah!" they shouted as the automobile began to move, pulling the trailer with it.

"Take care of Waggo if he comes back, and don't forget to mail the entry blank to the dog show," Bert added.

"I'll take care of everything, Master Bert, don't you fret," Dinah promised.

"I do hope Waggo comes home," said Flossie longingly, looking out the window.

The thought of their missing pet sobered the children for a little while. Soon they became interested in the sights along the road, and in watching the "house on wheels" behind them.

"Now it's a moving house," said Freddie, "and it can go just as fast as we can!"

Mr. Bobbsey made good time during the afternoon, since he was eager to cover as much ground as possible before they would have to stop for the night. Once Bert cried out:

"Dad! Dad! The trailer is coming loose! I can hear it!"

Mr. Bobbsey stopped and examined the connection. Everything was all right, but he decided not to put so much strain on the trailer. After that he drove more slowly.

For several hours they traveled through pretty farm country. The fields were bright with grain, and sleepy cows grazed in the pastures. Once the children caught sight of a mare with a long-legged colt at her heels.

"I want to get out and pet that horse and her baby!" cried Flossie.

Freddie said he guessed the colt's mother might have something to say about that. Everybody laughed. Then, before Daddy might have stopped, both the mare and her colt had galloped out of sight!

The Bobbseys had an early supper in a pretty little town. A little while after they had started on their way again, they came to land reserved as a trailer camp. The site was pleasantly located among trees near a small lake.

"Oh, let's stop here," begged Nan. "It would be such fun!"

"Yes, yes. Let's!" chorused the rest of the children.

"The only trouble is, we all can't sleep in the trailer," said Mother Bobbsey. "And without blankets we couldn't lie on the ground."

It was Tinky who discovered a pavilion almost hidden by the trees near the edge of the lake. "I reckon Mr. Bobbsey and us boys could stay thar," he suggested.

"Sure, that would be a good place if we had some cots," said Bert. "It would be kind of hard sleeping on the bare boards."

His father drew their attention to a farmhouse which could be seen dimly through the trees.

"Probably the man who owns this property lives there," he said. "Let's see what he can do for us in the way of cots."

They found the farmer and his wife very agreeable people. The couple were willing to furnish both cots and bedding.

"You can come up in the morning to breakfast if you like," the woman added. "We serve it when people want it."

"We'll be very glad to have it," said the twins' mother.

As soon as Daddy Bobbsey had pulled the trailer to a clear space near the water, everyone set to work making camp. They built a roaring fire and sat around it, singing songs. The farmer's wife brought a pitcher of milk and glasses to them. The fire made everyone drowsy, so it was not long before the travelers were ready to say good night.

"Trailer bedroom for girls!" laughed Bert.

"Come along, boys," said Mr. Bobbsey, leading the way toward the pavilion. "Bring your flashlights."

In the trailer Flossie and Nan whispered and

giggled for some time after Mother Bobbsey had put out the light. But gradually the clear air and the soft night sounds lulled them to sleep.

Sometime in the early morning, just as the birds began to twitter and chirp overhead, Freddie heard a gentle yip in his ear. Then he felt a cold, wet nose against his face. The little boy muttered something and turned over. His hand struck a warm, furry body. Instantly he was wide awake.

A small dog stood with its forepaws on the edge of Freddie's cot. It cocked its ear, barked, and tried to lick the little twin's face!

In the dim light, and only half-awake, Freddie at first mistook the dog for his own pet. He realized his mistake when he clasped the little animal in his arms.

"I th-thought you were Waggo!" he said.

Bert, awake now, whistled to the fox terrier. It frisked over to him, jumped up on his cot, and put up its right forepaw to shake hands.

"I suppose you've come from the farm to tell us it's time to get up," the boy laughed, starting a game of hide-and-seek.

He ducked under the blanket, and made the dog jump around and snoop, until it could find an opening to crawl under. The next thing Bert knew a cold, moist nose and a warm, wet tongue were tickling his feet!

"It's awful to get up!" said Freddie.

Daddy Bobbsey said it was just as well, as they had a long way to go that day. Tinky already was stirring. Soon they were dressed. The camp cots and bedding were folded neatly. Then the boys trudged up to the farmhouse to return the things, and to find out how soon breakfast would be ready.

"Oh, I want to help milk," cried Freddie, as he saw Farmer Jenkins going toward the barn with a large pail.

The little boy grabbed another bucket, which stood on a bench near the kitchen door. Happily he followed the man and asked if he might assist him.

"Well, son," the good-natured farmer smiled, "do you know anything about milking?"

"Y-yes," replied the little boy. "We've been on a farm. I think I remember how to milk."

Mr. Jenkins handed a small stool to the lad. Freddie sat down by the right side of a gentle-eyed bossy named Annabelle, put the pail between his knees, and started to work.

"You do know how," beamed the farmer, as a thin stream of milk splashed into the tin bucket. "Well, I'll go about my own job."

Freddie's hands were not very strong, so they soon grew tired. He was sure there were at least two glasses of milk in the pail, however—one for Flossie and one for himself.

Alas! When he looked, there was not a drop there! Everything had drained out through a hole. Some of the white fluid was on the little boy's socks and shoes, but most of it was running along the floor of the dairy barn.

"Never mind, I'll give you some from my pail," said Farmer Jenkins kindly when he saw how dismayed Freddie looked.

He poured out enough for two glasses into a good bucket, and the little boy proudly carried it to the house. Flossie was there.

"Oh, thank you," she said when she heard half the milk was for her. "I was just going to feed the chickens. Want to help?"

Off the two went and scattered the grain for the hens. Now it happened that there was a big rooster who stepped around haughtily and was not very friendly. Flossie thought he was taking more than his share of the food, so she tried to shoo him away.

Instantly she was sorry. The big bird raised himself up, spread his wings, then flew right at the little girl's face!

It was really Freddie who kept her from being pecked badly. At the moment the rooster made a dive at his twin, he ran into her and knocked her down. At the same instant came a shrill cry from a short distance away:

"Shoo! Shoo!"

Mrs. Jenkins hurried over and grabbed the big bird before he could injure anyone. Then she took the children into the house where breakfast soon made them forget their scare. She also directed their attention to neatly tied boxes of good things which Mrs. Bobbsey had ordered for a picnic lunch.

"Now we must pack up and hustle along,"

said Mr. Bobbsey as soon as they had finished eating.

"I'll fix the trailer," offered Nan, and skipped ahead of the others on a short cut to the camp grounds.

As she neared the lake, she stopped short. A man stood there, looking inside the trailer.

He was the thief!

Instantly the girl backed up, then turned and ran as fast as she could. Out of breath, she met the others coming across a field.

"The—the man who—took—the trailer," she gasped. "I—I think he's going to steal it again!"

Mr. Bobbsey, Bert and Tinky raced toward the lake, the rest of the family following them. When they arrived, no one was in sight, nor did anything seem to be missing from the trailer.

"Are you sure you saw the thief here?" asked Mr. Bobbsey. "The man wasn't Mr. Jenkins?"

"Oh, no," insisted Nan. "And if he was an honest person, why would he go away as soon as he heard us coming?"

This sounded reasonable. Mr. Bobbsey took his car and went up and down the highway, but he found nobody.

"If that thief is going South, we may find him yet," he said after the excitement had died down and the travelers were on their way again.

"It would have been dreadful if that man had taken my dresses," giggled Flossie, "and I'd have to wear this same one all the time!"

It was fun to be out on the highway once more.

Mr. Bobbsey drove steadily, while those with him pointed out objects of interest along the way. At noon he drew up at the side of the road not far from a stream and announced it was time for lunch.

"Here's a nice place," said Mrs. Bobbsey, walking to a spot among some trees.

"Let's have music with our meal," suggested Bert, bringing along Tinky's portable.

They had been back in the car and riding along merrily for nearly an hour when Nan suddenly asked, "Where's the portable, Bert?"

Her twin looked startled. "I don't know. But didn't anyone else pick it up?"

The radio had been forgotten!

CHAPTER X

LOST!

POOR Tinky! He was dreadfully upset, for he was sure he would never see his birthday present again.

"There's nothing to do but go back and look for the radio," said Daddy Bobbsey, stopping the car. "I'll take Nan with me and hunt for it. You boys watch over things here—and don't be forgetful again," he added firmly.

The trailer was driven into a grove of trees and detached from the Bobbsey car. Then Nan and her father went off in the automobile.

"Let's play house," suggested Flossie, who thought this was a good chance to have some fun in the trailer.

The bags and other things were lifted out, and in turn the children played Red Riding Hood, Cinderella, then older games like Noah's Ark. They had to stop this last one when Freddie forgot he was to find only sticks and stones that looked like animals. He brought in a big, live spider and a very long worm! As he went out he met his twin coming in.

"Here are some wild apples I found, Mother," said Flossie, dropping the fruit from the front of her skirt which she had used as a basket. "They're sour, though. They hurt my tongue."

Mother Bobbsey agreed to make an apple pie in the trailer's tiny oven. The "house on wheels" was very complete. Its little cupboard held everything necessary for cooking, for the children's mother had thought it best to stock it up in case they might not pass a restaurant.

"I'll need some ice cold water to make the crust," she said. "Did I hear someone say there is a spring near by?"

"I'd admire to git you some water, ma'am," offered Tinky, jumping up. "There's a fine fresh spring just over the next hill."

He and Bert went together, bringing a pailful. On the way back the Bobbsey boy told Tinky to go ahead with the bucket. He wanted to look at something in the next field.

"We're really in the South now," Bert said, "and I'd like to see what's different about it from where we live."

The first thing he saw he might have seen anywhere. And what happened to him might have happened any place, for a bad-tempered goat is the same the world over!

Bert had walked toward the brook which came from the spring. Maybe there were some fish in it different from any he had ever caught, he thought. As he stood listening to the gurgle of the stream and watching, he heard a sound behind him.

He turned, but not quickly enough to get out of the way. Something struck him, lifted him into the air, and tossed him to the other side of the brook.

"Oh! Ouch!" the boy cried out as he landed on the ground.

He sat up, but before he could arise, Bert saw a big white goat stepping through the water directly toward him. Quickly the lad took to his heels, but the animal could run just as fast as he could.

"Maa-a-a!" said the goat.

"Maa-a-a!" came an echo. "Maa-haa-maa haa!"

At the sound the animal stopped short, and Bert dared to look back. The call had not been an echo at all, but the voice of Tinky. The boy had seen what was happening to his friend and had rushed to help him.

"How'd you know what to do?" asked the Bobbsey twin, as the goat galloped off.

"Oh, my pa's been a-raisin' goats ever since I was a baby," Tinky replied. "I reckon I know their kind o' talk. Did he hurt you?"

"No," said Bert. "But I'm glad there was nice, soft grass along that brook!"

Meanwhile, Nan and her father were having their troubles trying to find the radio. In returning to the place where they had eaten the picnic lunch, they had taken the wrong road.

This had led them to an entirely strange section. Finally Mr. Bobbsey stopped the car and looked about him searchingly. He was lost!

"Do you recognize any of this?" he asked his daughter.

"There's a stream, and it looks something like the one where we had lunch," said Nan hopefully.

"Perhaps we are on the wrong side of it," said Mr. Bobbsey, frowning.

"I see a footbridge over there, Daddy," announced Nan, shading her eyes. "Let's see where it leads."

They left the car, and walked to the far side of the stream. Now the Bobbseys were standing only a few hundred feet from the place they were looking for. They did not know this, however. They turned their backs to the spot and wandered for some distance before realizing their mistake.

"I'm sure this is all wrong," called Mr. Bobbsey at last. "We seem to be getting farther and farther from the road. Come, Nan, let's go back."

At the footbridge they paused, uncertain whether to go to the car or to explore the stream in the opposite direction.

"We may as well look while we're here," said Nan. "I hope no one has stolen the radio," she added in alarm.

They had not taken many steps before the ground became familiar to them. They recognized an old, gnarled tree with long branches under which they had eaten.

"There's the radio!" cried Nan joyfully, running forward. "Just exactly where Bert and Tinky left it!"

Daddy Bobbsey, too, was glad. On their way to the car he laughed and said, "I trust we haven't forgotten where we left the automobile!"

He found it without any trouble. The radio was put on the seat between them, and the journey back to the trailer begun. On the way father and daughter talked about Waggo.

"Tomorrow morning I expect to call my office," Mr. Bobbsey said. "I'll ask about him," her father promised.

"I wonder if Susan Percy will be at the plantation when we get there," said Nan presently.

"I hope her family have found their heirlooms," Mr. Bobbsey spoke up. "It was very mysterious how a burglar could have taken them without the hunting dogs barking."

The mention of this made Nan think of another thief. She had not forgotten the person who had looked in the trailer that morning!

"Do you suppose we'll see that man again?" she asked.

"I don't know, but I hope the person who stole Mr. Hopper's trailer will be caught," replied her daddy. "Well, here we are back again," he added, as the rest of his family came into view and called out to them.

"Did you find the radio?" shouted Freddie and Flossie together.

"Yes, we did," responded Nan as the car came to a stop.

Tinky certainly was glad to see his present again, and he even insisted upon keeping it close to him when they stopped for the night. The following morning he became very excited—and also very worried. That very day he would arrive home. How would his parents greet him? Would they be very stern and punish him for running away?

"If I were your mother, I'd be so glad to see you I wouldn't do anything to you," said Nan, to whom he spoke about his fears.

Tinky hoped this would be the case, but he was very quiet as the travelers resumed their journey. Then suddenly he spoke up as he spied an airplane flying rather low. Mr. Bobbsey had stopped the automobile to give the twins their first view of growing cotton plants.

"I reckon you all better stay in the car," he cried out as Bert and Freddie started to get out. He pointed warningly overhead. "From up there he's fixin' to spray the fields to kill the bugs on the cotton. 'Tain't very pleasant for human folks."

Hurriedly the children closed the windows in the car and in the trailer. As they rode off quickly, Daddy Bobbsey explained that nowadays cotton fields are often sprayed with clouds of disinfectant from a plane.

"When a man has acres and acres of plants, it is the quickest way to reach the insects," he said.

"The worst bug is the boll weevil," said Tinky.

The Bobbsey Twins thought this was a hard name to remember, so their daddy said, "The boll is like the bud on a plant. And the weevil —well, he weaves his way in to eat up the boll."

"Does the dis-disfin-ectant kill the bugs?" asked Freddie thoughtfully.

"That's right, my Little Fireman," said Daddy Bobbsey.

Suddenly a dense fog of spray descended over the cotton fields on either side of the road. Daddy Bobbsey thought he was going to leave this behind. But alas, before he could get very far, there was a loud bang. A tire had blown out!

There was nothing to do but stop and wait until the airplane had finished its task. It was very hot in the car with the windows closed, so everyone was glad when at last the disinfectant had settled on the fields and fresh air could be let in again.

"Only the air isn't nice and sweet," said Flossie, "and the car is all splashed with white spots."

Daddy Bobbsey, Bert, and Tinky set about changing the tire. While this was going on, Freddie was thinking hard.

"My suit's made of cotton," he said to himself. "I wonder if there are any little weevils in it." Finding a tiny hole in one sleeve, he decided there must be. "Yes, something is eating this!" he stated firmly.

Without saying a word to anyone, he went into the trailer to find a small sprayer. To this was attached a can holding colorless liquid to kill flies and mosquitoes.

Pfuff, pfuff, pfuff went Freddie, turning a stream of the smelly stuff onto his clothes. He kept this up until his eyes began to water and he started to sneeze. Then he put away the sprayer and joined his family.

"Freddie Bobbsey!" cried his mother as soon as she got a whiff of him. "What *have* you been doing?"

He told her. Then, as she marched him back to the trailer to change his clothes, she told him that weevils attacked only growing cotton.

As the afternoon wore on, they passed more cotton fields. Once they caught a glimpse of a gin where Daddy Bobbsey said the raw cotton was brought to have the seeds and dust taken out of it.

"I'll tell you more about a gin some day when we visit one," he promised, "but there isn't time now. Tinky," he added, "isn't your place somewhere near here?"

During the past hour the Southern boy had been growing more and more restless. Now he said in a voice tense with excitement:

"Pa's farm lies jest t'other side the next ridge!"

CHAPTER XI

STRANGE BEDS

SO Tinky was almost home!

The twins were nearly as excited as he was when they topped the next ridge and looked down into the valley.

"There! There's a farmhouse!" exclaimed Bert. "Is that it, Tinky? Is that where you live?"

"That's it—that's my home," eagerly replied the little lad from the Land of Cotton.

Below them lay a small farm. The house and barns needed paint, but the fences had been mended and the drive was free of weeds.

"There's Pa!" cried Tinky.

Near the house was a man sawing wood. He was thin and slightly stooped, and wore faded overalls. He straightened as the Bobbsey car turned in from the highway.

Tumbling out and running to meet the hurrying figure, the boy cried, "Oh, Pa, I shouldn't ought to've run off! You ain't goin' to hold it agin me, air you?"

"There, there, what's done is done," said the man in blue denim, clumsily patting the lad's shoulder. "Reckon you've learned your lesson. Best we forgit it, now you're back."

The door of the farmhouse opened. The next moment someone whom the boy called "Ma" had clasped the runaway in her arms, and was laughing and crying over him.

"Oh, Tinky lad, it's good to have you home again!" his mother stated joyfully.

Finally the boy remembered to introduce Mr. and Mrs. Bobbsey and the two sets of twins. All were made welcome by Mr. and Mrs. Racher.

"Reckon you was good to my Tinky, so you and us should be friends," the woman said, shaking hands.

"You're as welcome as our own folks would be," smiled the runaway's father, asking them to come inside.

"They gave me a present for my birthday, Pa," continued his son. "Reckon you'll be s'prised."

"What be it?"

"A real talkin' box."

"What do you mean?"

"A radio," explained Nan, "for entertainment."

Tinky produced the wonderful gift, and soon sweet music from it filled the old house. When the program ended, Mrs. Racher spoke up kindly, eager to make the newcomers welcome.

"We'd admire to have you for as long as you kin stay. Tinky, fetch out all their bags."

"Thank you," said Mrs. Bobbsey, "but I believe we ought to go along," she added, looking at the small rooms, and figuring there would be no place for them all to sleep.

"Please stay," added Tinky, looking at Mr. Bobbsey. "You promised to look over Pa's woods."

"Yes, I'm in the lumber business in Lakeport," explained the twins' father to the farmer, "and I might buy some of your trees."

"I'd admire to show them to you," Tinky's father replied, pleased. "You certainly got to stay a night or two."

The problem of where to sleep was finally decided. Mother Bobbsey and the girls would stay in the house, while Freddie and his father would use the trailer. Bert and Tinky would sleep in the haymow.

It was fun fixing this place for the night. The boys piled up clean, sweet hay, bunching it up at one end to form a pillow. Over this they spread a blanket. Freddie thought it would be more enjoyable to be with the boys, but Daddy Bobbsey said the little twin better sleep with him.

"I'd be lonesome all by myself." He laughed. "Anyway, one of the horses might get hungry in the night and pull your bed right from underneath you!"

The travelers were so tired that they probably could have slept most anywhere. They were up early, though, and were ready to see the Racher place.

Mr. Bobbsey went with the owner to inspect the trees in the forest. Bert and Tinky joined the men after doing several chores. The small twins stayed near the house to play. Presently Tinky's mother came outside with a basket of trash.

"I burn my rubbish over yonder," Mrs. Racher explained to Freddie and Flossie as they followed her.

"We'll help you set fire to it," cried the little boy. "I love to play fireman."

Mrs. Racher entered into the fun. "If you like to do that, I'll show you how to play fire in the mountains, where we don't have no engines," she said.

She built a small make-believe log cabin out of sticks and twigs. To each of the twins she gave a little bucket and told them where to find a brook.

"When this playhouse starts a-burnin'," she smiled, "you fetch some water fast as you kin run. Thet's the way we do it here in the country," she added, going into the woodshed for a moment.

Flossie did not realize that Mrs. Racher actually was going to put a match to the little house. She thought the woman was going to burn only the trash. To make the game seem more real, the little girl put her precious doll inside the log cabin.

"All ready!" Tinky's mother said. "Go over to the garden, count up to fifty, then look back. You'll know how to play the rest."

The twins did this. Finally Freddie called,

"Fifty! Whoops! *Fire!*" and ran toward the brook.

But Flossie just stood and stared. The cabin was really in flames and inside it was her doll!

Sobbing, she hurried to Mrs. Racher and told her what the trouble was. The toy was pulled out quickly and, though black with soot, was unharmed. Relieved, Flossie went off to scrub the doll.

Freddie, meanwhile, kept dousing the fire until it was out. "I had lots of fun," he told his daddy when the men returned for lunch.

They were busy talking about the trees, and the little boy heard Mr. Bobbsey say he would like to buy a lot of Mr. Racher's timber.

"I like your lumber, and I can use a good bit of it. I'm surprised you haven't sold more of it," were his words.

"I never had a way to git out the wood," Tinky's father replied. "The farm just pays me a livin', so I never had any money to buy tools or haul out the logs."

Mr. Bobbsey thought for a moment, then said, "I'll pay you for your wood, and send men and machines in here at my expense to cut down the trees I want."

"Pa, that's great," said Tinky. "I reckon you'll be rich now."

Mrs. Racher was equally delighted, and began to plan at once how she might buy things needed for her house.

"I kin have the easy chair and curtains for the front room I've wanted so long," she said. "An' Tinky an' me an' Pa kin have better clothes. Reckon you folks must be angels, sort of, to bring so much happiness to a body."

Flossie thought this over a minute, then asked, "Do you think angels' daughters could be called fairies? Daddy calls me Fat Fairy."

Everyone laughed at this, then they sat down to lunch. During the meal the Rachers heard for the first time why the Bobbseys had come to the Land of Cotton, and how they happened to be bringing the stolen trailer with them.

"My, my, when I think o' Tinky a-ridin' along with a thief, it makes me shiver," said the boy's mother.

"He never seed me," her son spoke up.

"I reckon that's lucky," said Mr. Racher. "I'll keep a-hopin' the police catch him."

Suddenly Nan sat up very straight in her chair. "I just thought of something! Maybe that man stole our pet!" she said.

"That's right," added Bert. "Perhaps he had Waggo in his car that time when you saw him looking in the trailer, Nan."

This idea made all the twins glum for a while, so Tinky tried to cheer them up by asking them if they would like to take a walk in the woods.

"Be mighty careful o' the bog," his mother warned. "Make the Bobbseys stay to the paths."

The boy promised, then explained that if a person got into certain oozy, muddy places he sometimes had hard work getting out.

"Good-bye, good-bye," called the twins happily as they left the farmhouse.

The big woods was a lovely place. There were bright-colored birds, and ferns and flowers of varieties which the Northern children never had seen.

"Let's chase a butterfly," cried Flossie, darting after a big yellow one.

A little later they came upon a clump of beautiful blossoms growing close to swampy ground. Nan said:

"Oh, I'd love to pick some of them for Mother. Would it be safe for us to walk there, Tinky?"

"Reckon I kin get you a few," replied the boy,

advancing slowly along over the soft ground.

The twins watched, fascinated, as he made his way. Each step was tested before he dared to bear his weight on the soil. Even then the muddy water welled up here and there.

"Oh, come back, Tinky. It's too risky. Please come back!" Nan called anxiously.

But Tinky reached the clump of flowers, picked a few and made his way back in safety.

The older Bobbsey girl thanked him and accepted the bouquet. They were going on when suddenly she exclaimed:

"Where's Freddie?"

"Why, he was here just a minute ago," spoke up Bert.

"He went over there," said Flossie, pointing with a chubby finger. "I think he wanted to get some flowers, too."

Nan looked at Tinky. "Is it very dangerous —in that direction?" she asked.

"Reckon 'tain't exactly safe," the boy replied.

Already he was running forward, the Bobbseys just behind him.

"Freddie, where are you? Freddie! Freddie!" Nan cried out.

At last the children thought they heard a faint, answering call. They stood still and listened.

Yes, there it was again! No doubt about it, this time. It was Freddie's voice!

Then they saw him. The little boy was knee-deep in the sucking mud, and sinking fast!

Freddie was so frightened that all he could do

was stare at them and hold out his arms. Nan and Bert wanted to rush in to rescue him, but Tinky held them back.

"No, no!" he cried. "You'd be pulled under. Reckon there ain't no time to lose, though. Do just as I say."

Under his guidance the three older children broke down a slender sapling by bending it far over, then jumping on the trunk until it was broken through. It was not easy, because the young tree was tough. Finally it snapped off.

"What do we do now?" asked Nan.

"Use it as a pole," answered Tinky. "But we need two."

"We'll come soon, Freddie," Nan called out. She tried to sound calm, but she was shaking with fear.

Another sapling was broken in the same way. Though the three worked fast, and Flossie tried to help, it seemed forever before they were ready to use the slender trees. Freddie was sunken almost to his waist now, his eyes filled with tears.

"Reckon ef we kin git these poles under his arms, he'll be all right," said Tinky. "Freddie, hold on to these," the boy ordered as he and Bert slid the two saplings across the bog, putting the ends on firm ground.

Freddie did not obey. He was too frightened to do anything but sob as he sank still lower.

CHAPTER XII

THE BOG

TINKY'S plan to get the two saplings under Freddie's arms so that he could save himself had to be given up. The little boy was too scared to do anything. Another scheme must be thought of—and thought of quickly.

"I'll get him," offered Bert, stepping onto one of the poles.

"No, no, it'll roll with ye!" cried Tinky. "I'll slip across. Nan and Flossie, you hold the ends of the poles on this side. I'll hold t'other. Then, Bert, you hitch across on your stomach and get Freddie."

The poles were laid about two feet apart, on one side of Freddie, with the ends on rocky ground. Using the saplings as a footbridge, Tinky scampered across them, landing safely on the other side. He took a firm grip of the pole ends, while Nan and Flossie seized those on the path.

Now it was time for Bert's part. Lying flat, he began to worm himself sideways across the two poles.

"Be there in a minute, Freddie," he grunted encouragingly.

The saplings bent under the boy's weight, and bubbles formed as the mud sucked at them. But Bert kept on. His little brother, sunken now to his armpits, began to struggle.

"Keep still! Don't move at all until I tell you to," Bert ordered.

Inch by inch he crawled along until he was opposite Freddie. Then he said:

"Do just what I say. Put your arms around my neck. That's right," he said as the little fellow's arms gripped him hard. "Now hold on tight, and don't let go, whatever you do. Understand?"

"All r-right," said Freddie.

"Now I'm going to start back slowly. Try to work yourself out of the mud as we go. Ready?"

"R-ready!" agreed his small brother.

The bog had a terrible hold on the little fellow. For a moment it seemed to Bert that Freddie must be held down with bands of steel. He did not dare to put too much pressure on the saplings, for fear one or both of them might break. He could not use his hands to help his brother without taking the chance of being pulled into the bog himself. For several seconds it seemed as if they could make no progress, either forward or backward.

"Freddie, you've got to come back!" cried Flossie.

The small lad heard his twin and tried

harder. This time he was able to pull himself up a little.

"That's it. I think we've got it. Now hang on, Freddie, while I move a little!" cried Bert.

It was hard, slow work, but finally Freddie was pulled up, so his body lay on top of the mud. He put one hand on the nearest pole and with Bert's help was able to lie across the two saplings as Bert was doing.

"Oh, Freddie's safe!" cried Flossie joyfully.

Their troubles were not over yet, though. The Bobbsey boys had nearly reached firm ground, when one of the saplings snapped. The feet of Bert and Freddie sank in the mud!

Quickly Nan reached over and grabbed each of her brothers by an arm. Flossie grasped her twin's hair! Between them they helped the boys to safety.

"That's a right good job!" came a voice. There was Tinky, still on the far side of the bog, grinning at them.

"Oh, I'd forgotten poor Tinky, and after he did so much to help us!" Nan exclaimed. "How is he ever going to get back?"

There now was only one good pole over the boggy spot, and this was covered with slimy, slippery mud!

"Maybe I'd better go to the farm and get a ladder, Tinky," Bert called to him. "We could lay that across and you'd make it easy."

"Reckon I kin make it, anyways," the lad replied. "Jest see you hold firm your end is all."

The Bobbseys were very careful to do this. Anxiously the twins watched Tinky measure the distance with his woodsman's eye. Then he took a running start and launched himself on the dangerous bridge.

A moment more and it was done. Tinky reached the end of the sapling and eager hands stretched out to draw him to safety.

When the excitement was over, Nan suddenly realized how very dirty they all were. "Our folks will wonder what we've been doing," she said.

"They—they told me to stay on the path," added Freddie sorrowfully.

"You should have, too," said Flossie.

Bert felt that his little brother should tell the story in his own way. Nan gave him the flowers which Tinky had gathered to hand to his mother. Actually Freddie had got himself in trouble in his desire to pick some for her.

Mrs. Bobbsey certainly was astonished to see her young son, covered with mud, holding out a gift to her. Before she could speak, he told everything that had happened. He did not forget to praise the other children, especially Bert and Tinky. The Southern mountain boy was very much embarrassed.

"I didn't do much," he insisted. "Um, I reckon Ma's got a good dinner cooking," he added to change the subject.

"I went a-huntin' this afternoon and got a few birds," explained Mr. Racher.

"We ain't had dove pie for a long time," his wife said. "Reckon Pa must have knowed we wanted somethin' a little extry special tonight for the Bobbseys."

The twins had never eaten dove pie before, but they learned a little later that it was very tasty. When Nan passed her plate for a second helping, she said laughingly:

"This must be something like the blackbird pie that was set before the king!"

"But those blackbirds were supposed to sing," teased her daddy. "Doves can only coo."

Everyone laughed, and the dinner made a merry kind of ending to the visit of the Bobbseys.

"We must leave early in the morning," said the twins' father as they left the table.

By seven o'clock the travelers were on their way. During the morning they saw many cotton fields—so many, in fact, that Bert wondered what would be done with all the cotton.

Mr. Bobbsey said, "Many, many things are made from it, either in whole, or in part; things like hammocks, dolls, boxing gloves, automobile tires—"

"Did you say automobile tires, Dad?" Bert asked. "I thought they were made of rubber."

"Not entirely," replied his father. "Other things are mixed with that. I believe there is a special kind of cotton, called pima, which helps to make very strong tires."

"Golly, I guess there must be cotton in just about everything!" Freddie cried out.

"Not quite," laughed Daddy Bobbsey, "but some people have said it's just about as good as money in the bank."

"I once heard a story about that," Mother Bobbsey added. "It was about a farmer who kept bales of cotton in his barn instead of selling them. Whenever he needed a little money, he would take a few bales into town and get cash for them. He said the cotton was as good as money in the bank and it saved him the fuss of having an account!"

Nan said she thought this was a little dangerous. "Suppose the farmer's barn had burned, then where would he have been?"

"Where, indeed?" agreed Daddy Bobbsey. "Probably he never thought of that."

"Oh, look!" cried Freddie, pointing to a man who was plowing between rows of cotton plants. "He has a mule!"

The twins begged their father to stop the car, and piled out. The planter, a pleasant man with friendly eyes, waved as they walked over. He pushed his hat to the back of his head and clucked to the mule, who promptly sat down in the middle of a half-plowed row.

"This old mule's bashful—Jonathan just won't work in front of strangers." The farmer grinned good-naturedly. The Bobbseys laughed at this and before they left, the man handed each twin a green cotton boll.

"These bolls start out as pretty yellow flowers," he explained. "When the flowers drop off, the boll bursts and old King Cotton pops up inside. Then he goes off to the gin to be cleaned."

The children thanked him and the family drove on to the next town. Here they found a celebration was going on, so Mr. Bobbsey stopped the car.

As he did, two men came across the crowded street and looked into the trailer. Then one of them wrote something on a piece of paper. Only Nan noticed this, as she was looking out the rear window of the automobile. But before she could tell her father about it, they were all startled by several loud blasts on a trumpet. The crowd rushed forward.

"Oh, let's go!" cried Bert.

As the Bobbseys got out of their car, they spied a man high on the roof of the general store. He put a horn to his mouth and blew another loud blast.

"Friends and fellow citizens," he cried, as the crowd quieted, "I have the pleasure to announce to you all that we are about to have a Turkey Trot." Cheers came from the crowd. "We will release several live turkeys—very much alive, I can assure you!"

"Why is he going to do that, Daddy?" asked Freddie.

"Listen!" replied his father.

"Each one of these turkeys," the man continued, "will have a slip attached to its leg. On each one will be an order for a prize at our store. Your job," he added with a laugh, "will be to catch the turkeys!"

Another man beside him opened a crate.

While the Bobbsey children watched, a large

turkey gobbler was tossed from the roof. With a good deal of squawking and wing-flapping, it fluttered down among the crowd.

Another turkey and still another followed, while the people darted about with shouts and laughter, making frantic attempts to capture the big birds. What fun!

Suddenly one old gobbler made straight for Freddie. The little fellow reached out to grab it, not realizing that the big, strong bird meant to peck him.

"Oo!" screamed Flossie.

Just in time Mother Bobbsey pulled her little son out of harm's way. With a squawk the big gobbler sailed past them.

At last all the birds were captured, and those who had got them went into the store to claim their prizes. The Bobbseys went in, too, as the children begged to buy some things especially made in the Land of Cotton.

"I want some sugar cane candy," said Flossie.

While Mrs. Bobbsey made the purchases—among them sunbonnets and sugar cane candy for the little twins—the others watched the prize winners get hams, sacks of flour, overalls, garden rakes, and other useful articles. Nan noticed two men in the crowd who whispered together and from time to time glanced at her father in an unfriendly way.

"They are the same ones who wrote down something after they looked at the trailer," she thought.

CHAPTER XIII

GREASED PIGS

NAN went over to tell her daddy about the unfriendly men, but he was busy, and she did not want to interrupt him. While she was waiting, Flossie came running to her.

"A man is here to take our picture," said the little girl, "on a watermelon."

Nan could not guess what her sister was talking about, but she followed her to the porch of the country store. There stood a very tall, thin man in a black suit. He had a long mustache which curled down at the ends. Near him was a camera on a tripod with a black cloth over it.

"You're from the No'th," he said, smiling. "You ought to have a real Southern picture of yourself. Now, miss," he told Nan, "you sit on that melon there, and I'll take a snapshot of you."

Looking around, the older Bobbsey girl saw a watermelon that she was sure was the biggest one that ever grew. If stood on end, it would have been almost as high as her little sister.

"Do you carry this with you to take pictures on?" Flossie asked the photographer.

The man laughed. "Oh, no, that belongs to the storekeeper. But he'll let you sit on it."

Nan asked how much the photographer would charge, and when she found out it was only twenty-five cents for one picture, she decided to let him take it. She would now have something different to show to Nellie Parks and her other chums in Lakeport.

"All ready," said the man. "Little girl," he added, meaning Flossie, "stand alongside your sister with one hand on her shoulder."

She did as directed. Just as the photographer finished, Freddie came bursting through the screen door, slamming it so hard that it hit the wall with a bang. Seeing his sister on the watermelon, and the man with the camera, he cried:

"Oh, I want my picture taken, too!"

He rushed toward Nan and plumped himself squarely into her lap. Now the melon was strong enough for Nan to sit on alone. But Freddie's weight, added to hers—and added with such force—was too much. The big green fruit broke open with a swishing noise. Down went brother and sister together on top of a mass of crushed pink pulp and juice.

"Oh, Freddie!" cried Nan. "You've ruined the watermelon!"

"And spoiled your clothes too," said Mrs. Bobbsey. "Freddie, how *do* you get into so much mischief?"

While Mr. Bobbsey paid the storekeeper for the melon, the photographer gave the twins two finished pictures. One was of Nan on the watermelon, with Flossie alongside, the other of Nan and Freddie in the smashed fruit. They were so good that Mr. Bobbsey bought them both.

As Nan and Freddie, with their mother, went back to the trailer to change clothes, Bert noticed a large crowd gathering in the public square.

"Let's see what's going on, Dad," he suggested, and the three Bobbseys hurried over.

Part of the public square had been cleared. In the center of this, enclosed in a wire coop, were a number of highly polished, squealing pigs.

"Ooh, what are they going to do with them?" cried Flossie. "I hope they aren't

going to throw them from a roof like the turkeys, 'cause they haven't any wings."

Her daddy laughed. "I hope not too, because I never heard of a flying pig!"

The next moment a wild shout from the square told them that the game was about to begin. A man standing next to the Bobbseys explained it to them.

"The pigs have had grease rubbed all over them. They are very slippery. That makes it hard for folks to catch them."

"Can you keep one if you catch it?" asked Bert.

"Yes, indeed," the man replied. "The pigs are given as prizes by the town. We have this celebration once a year."

"We came through on just the right day," said Daddy Bobbsey. "My children have never been in the Land of Cotton before, and they are learning a lot about this section of our country."

"We love it," added Flossie.

"The porkers are out!" someone shouted.

Such a scramble! Men running here and there. Boys shouting. Pigs squealing shrilly.

It was not easy to catch the slippery animals. Again and again one would seem to be captured, but would slip through the hands of the man who thought he had hold of a prize. At last, though, all were caught but one. This fellow, larger and more determined than the rest, broke away and dashed into the crowd. It came straight toward the Bobbseys!

"Look out!" cried the twins' father.

He stepped out of the way just in time. Bert was not so lucky. He tried to dodge, but was hemmed in by the crowd. The pig hit him a glancing blow which made him lose his balance and fall into the gutter. He was not hurt, but he was embarrassed.

"To think an old pig could knock me down!" he said in disgust.

The prize finally was caught, and the crowd began to leave. It had been an exciting day.

Nan and Freddie appeared in fresh clothes, and the family climbed into the Bobbsey car. They made slow progress through the street, for the trailer took up a lot of space. Many heads were turned as they passed, and once two men pointed after them curiously.

"We seem to be attracting a great deal of attention. Evidently trailers are a novelty around here," said Daddy Bobbsey.

Nan was uneasy, and told about the unfriendly men.

"They just pointed at us," she said. "A little while ago they were talking about you in the store. Before that they wrote down something about the trailer."

Mr. Bobbsey was thoughtful for several seconds. Then he said he was sure it could mean nothing.

"Aren't we going to give the trailer back to the one who owns it soon, Daddy?" asked Flossie.

"Pretty soon, Fat Fairy. It won't be long now before we get to Great Oaks plantation," he answered. "Mr. Hopper lives near it. I guess he'll be glad to have his trailer again."

This set the children to wondering who the man could be who had stolen it, and whether or not the police had found him yet. For some time after they had left the village far behind, they talked about this.

"A trailer is kind of a funny thing to steal. It's so big, and you can't hide it anywhere," observed Freddie.

"The Hoppers were away and did not know it was gone until they got home," said Mother Bobbsey. "Probably the thief hoped to sell the trailer before the police knew it was gone."

"Maybe he stole other things that he wanted to hide," said Bert thoughtfully. "The trailer would have been a good way to get such things out of town!"

Suddenly there was the sound of a police siren on the road behind them. Mr. Bobbsey drew over to let the car pass by. To his surprise, the driver pulled up beside him and gave the signal to stop.

"Well, what can I do for you, officer?" asked Mr. Bobbsey pleasantly.

He was completely surprised by the reply.

"You can come with me, if you please. You're under arrest."

CHAPTER XIV

IN TROUBLE

"UNDER arrest!" gasped the Bobbseys.

"There must be some mistake, officer," added the twins' father.

"It's no mistake that the trailer you've got behind your car there is stolen property," said the policeman. He was kind, but it was plain from his manner that he was not a person to be trifled with! "It was recognized and reported a couple of towns back."

"Those mean men! They must have been detectives!" cried Nan.

"It's true the trailer was stolen," said Mr. Bobbsey. "But if you check up on your records, you will find that I am not the thief. I am merely taking it to the owner."

"I'd like to believe your story," said the man in the police car, "but duty is duty. My orders are to bring you to the sheriff's office."

Never dreaming that more trouble lay ahead, Mr. Bobbsey followed the officer into the next town and parked in front of Headquarters. The whole family followed him inside, and also a curious little boy who had seen them drive up.

"These are the people with the stolen trailer," reported the officer who had stopped them on the road.

The sheriff at once asked for Mr. Bobbsey's driver's license, and those for his car and the trailer. Of course, Mr. Bobbsey did not have the one for the "house on wheels," but he explained that it belonged to Mr. Hopper.

"That's the name I have on record," said the sheriff. "Also, I have orders to pick up the person who took the trailer."

"But I didn't take it," argued Mr. Bobbsey. "The Lakeport police asked me to bring it along, since I was coming South anyway."

"That story hasn't been sent around," said the sheriff. "First I've heard it."

"It's true," cried Bert, who did not like the fact that the man did not seem to believe his daddy. "My brother and sisters and I saw the mean person who stole the trailer. He was right in Lakeport. And the other day Nan saw him again. I'll bet he's around here somewhere this very minute!"

"He has a big nose, and my daddy hasn't," said Flossie.

This remark made the sheriff laugh. "I must admit your father does not look like a thief," he said, "but it's my job to enforce the law. Mr. Bobbsey, I must hold both your car and the trailer until I check up on your story."

There was nothing more the twins' father

could say. He was annoyed by the delay, but it was not the fault of this officer. In fact, the sheriff suggested a place where the Bobbseys might enjoy an overnight stay.

"Just walk along this street for two blocks and you'll see a big brick house," he said. "Mrs. Rolt, who lives there, sometimes takes tourists."

While Daddy and Mother Bobbsey talked this over, the little boy who had followed them into the building, ran outside. No one had noticed him, but he had heard every word that had been said.

"I'm going to tell my mama about this," he said to himself as he ran home. "Those people are thieves!"

Unaware that anyone in the town except the police would know why the Bobbseys had to remain, the parents of the twins decided to go to the Rolt home.

"Suppose I walk up there alone," suggested Mr. Bobbsey, "and see about rooms."

In the end Nan and the little twins went with him. Several minutes passed after they had knocked at the door before Mrs. Rolt opened it a little way.

"How do you do?" said Mr. Bobbsey pleasantly. "I'd like to find out about rooms for my family. We'll need three—"

"I can't accommodate you," the woman said tartly, starting to close the door.

"Then can you tell me where I might find a place?" asked the twins' father.

"No, I can't," came the quick reply. "I don't know of a soul who would take you in."

Mrs. Rolt closed the door and locked it. Then she smiled at her small son Jimmy, who had run from the sheriff's office to tell her that the Bobbseys had stolen a trailer!

On the outside of the house the children and their father, surprised at such a reception, stood talking a moment. Suddenly Freddie's attention was drawn to a small building in the garden of the property next to the Rolts.

"Gee, Floss, it's a playhouse!" he cried, dashing away. "Let's look at it!"

The twins ran off together to inspect the place. It was the prettiest make-believe house the twins had ever seen. It had a sloping roof, latticed windows, and a real door that opened when the knob was turned.

"It's exactly like a fairy house," said Flossie, clapping her hands.

The twins just peeked inside. They would not do more without permission. A tiny room was furnished with a child's table, chairs, desk and a stove.

"Do you think it's enchanted, Freddie?" asked his twin, who liked to act out the stories she read. "Maybe it's the castle of the Sleeping Princess—the one in the fairy story."

"No, it's just a playhouse," said Freddie, looking about the ground outside in the hope of finding footprints. When he found none, he added, "I guess nobody uses it."

Suddenly the little boy saw something bright gleaming in a near-by bush and pounced upon it eagerly.

"Look what I found!" he cried. "It's a pin, and a pretty one, too. It's got printing on the other side."

At this moment Nan joined her brother and sister. Daddy Bobbsey had sent her over to bring the twins back to the sheriff's office. He had started for the place already.

"Can you read what this says?" asked Freddie, handing what he had found to Nan.

"It's a school pin," she replied. "Miss—Miss Palmer's School for Girls. Why, that's the one our cousin Susan Percy went to."

"Maybe the girl who lost this one lives here," said Flossie.

"Prob'bly this is her playhouse," added Freddie.

"Only now she must be too old to use it," decided Nan. "Let's go to the big house and ask about the pin."

A beautiful lady with gray hair came to the door when they knocked. She smiled at the children.

"We found this," spoke up Freddie, handing her the school pin.

"Oh, I'm so glad! This belongs to my daughter. Before she went away, she searched for it everywhere."

"We have a cousin who attended that school," said Nan. "Her name is Susan Percy."

"Susan Percy, the daughter of Colonel and Mrs. Percy of Great Oaks? Why, she and my Alice are great friends," said the woman. "Do come in, children, and tell me about yourselves. You're from the North, aren't you? Our name is Clay."

"Thank you," said Nan, "but our parents are waiting for us."

"We have to stay in this town all night," spoke up Flossie, "but we can't find any place to sleep!"

Nan thought it best to tell the whole story.

"Why, the idea," said Mrs. Clay, after hearing everything, even the part about her next door neighbor. "I'll go right down to the sheriff's office with you. Of course he has to enforce the law, but I'd be sorry to have you go away not liking our town. You are going to spend the night with me!"

So that was how it happened that the Bobbseys stayed with the friendly woman until the next morning. They learned that the daughter, who used to play in the little house in the garden, had now graduated from Miss Palmer's School. At the present time she was in New York, having been a bridesmaid at a wedding.

"The same one our Cousin Susan Percy went to!" exclaimed Nan when she heard the name of the bride.

By morning the sheriff had received the telegrams for which he had been waiting. The Bobbseys could leave any time, he said, since he had found their story to be true. Mr. Bobbsey now did not regret the delay, as Mrs. Clay had sent him to see a man who had some fine old pine boards. He had bought every one of them for the Washington House in Lakeport.

"Before we go," the twins' father told his family, "I must telephone to my office about this purchase."

"Find out about Waggo, please," Flossie begged. "Last time you called he wasn't back, but maybe he is now."

The little girl was to be disappointed, and also her brothers and sister. Nothing had been learned about Waggo.

"All I care about is having him back," said Nan. "But it would have been fun putting him in the show."

"I bet he'd get a prize," spoke up Freddie loyally.

Again the children wondered if the little fox terrier might be in the possession of the man who stole the trailer. The sheriff had told them the thief had not been caught yet.

"I still think maybe he took the trailer to put in other things he stole," said Bert to Nan a few minutes later when they were alone.

"I have an idea!" cried his twin sister. "Oh, why didn't I think of it before?"

"What is it?" questioned the boy.

"Nobody ever asked Tinky whether anything was in the trailer," Nan replied.

"That's right," said Bert excitedly. "Let's

write a letter to him right away and find out."

"This very minute," agreed Nan, hurrying off to find Mrs. Clay.

The kindly woman gave them paper and envelope. In a few minutes they had written the note which she promised to mail for them, as Daddy Bobbsey was out in front waiting to start.

"Good-bye, and thank you so much," said Nan.

"You've been awfully nice to us," added Bert.

The Bobbseys waved to Mrs. Clay as the car and the trailer rolled down the street. Then they became interested in the countryside. Here and there was a large field of growing hemp.

"You'd never think a person could make rope out of that, would you?" asked Bert.

"No, it doesn't look anything like it now," agreed Daddy Bobbsey. "By the way, I have a surprise for you."

"What is it?" cried all four children together.

"We have to stop at a town we'll come to in about half an hour," he replied.

Flossie was disappointed. "That's not much of a s'prise. We've been stopping all the time," she said.

Her father laughed. "But this will be a special kind of stop," he told her. "The police there are holding a man who they think may have stolen this trailer. They want the Bobbsey Twins to identify him!"

CHAPTER XV

GREAT OAKS

AT THIS announcement the children became very excited. They felt very important, too.

"Won't it be wonderful if the man should turn out to be the right one?" cried Nan.

"I hope we 'member him," said Flossie.

"I'd never forget him," replied Bert. "And I know his voice, too."

For the next half hour the Bobbsey Twins could hardly sit still. When they finally reached the pretty little town where their father was going to stop, Freddie stood up and sang out:

"I want to go first!"

His mother thought it best if only Nan and Bert went inside the police station with Daddy Bobbsey. She promised the little twins that if the prisoner should be the thief, then she might let them talk to the chief. They soon became interested in the people and the houses of the town, so the time passed quickly. It seemed only a few minutes before Freddie spied the others coming back.

"Now let me ask Daddy," he begged, so his

mother opened the car door. "Is he? Does it? Can we?" cried the little boy, grasping his father's hand.

Mr. Bobbsey smiled at his small son. "Sorry, Little Fireman," he said, "but the person inside doesn't seem to be the one we're looking for."

The twins were disappointed, but would not give up hope. "I'm going to catch that bad man yet!" announced Freddie stoutly as they got into the automobile.

After they had ridden along for some time, the Bobbseys began to think about Great Oaks plantation, for it would not be long now before they would reach it.

"I wonder if it looks like Susan says," spoke up Nan. "It sounded so beautiful."

"If I can have a horse to ride, it'll be swell," added Bert.

They were passing through historic country now. More than once Mr. Bobbsey stopped the car so that they might read the tablets on houses and in parks. These told of some stirring action during the Civil War, or showed where some brave soldier had lost his life.

"Golly, I never knew we had so many heroes," said Freddie after one of these stops. "America's a fine country to live in, isn't it, Daddy?"

"Yes, indeed, and don't you ever forget it," said Mr. Bobbsey heartily. "And now, children, keep your eyes open. This road leads directly to Great Oaks."

A few moments more and they saw the house! It was exactly as Susan had pictured it to them.

"Only it's even more beautiful than she said it was," Nan commented.

The large white house had long columns that reached from the porch to the roof. Giant trees spread their sheltering branches over the roof, making the rooms below cool on hot days.

A stone wall, not very high, set off the lawn from the road. Over its top grew rambler roses, the kind which bloom all summer. Some of the flowers were pink, others white. Back of the house the children caught a glimpse of other large buildings, which they supposed were the stables.

"And over there," said Mrs. Bobbsey, pointing to the other side of the road, "are the cabins of the plantation workers."

"Aren't they cute?" cried Flossie, bouncing back onto the seat.

She had been standing up, but now she sat back *kerplunk,* for Daddy Bobbsey had turned the car into the broad drive leading to the house.

A little Negro boy saw them coming. He stared open-mouthed for a moment, then scuttled around to the back of the house, probably to give warning of their arrival.

Consequently, the Bobbseys had barely stopped their car when the front door opened and Mrs. Percy came out to greet them.

"How glad we are to see you!" she said, kissing Mother Bobbsey and opening her arms wide to the twins. "The Colonel and I have been watching the roads all day. We were beginning to be afraid something had detained you."

"Many things made us late, Martha," laughed the children's mother. "We are so glad to be here."

The twins regarded their cousin with lively interest. She had white hair, but a young-looking face. Her figure was slim and she had lovely, sparkling black eyes that reminded them of Susan. They liked her at once.

"Is our Cousin Susan here?" asked Flossie.

"No, she hasn't returned yet, but we expect her soon," smiled the young woman's mother.

A moment later Colonel Percy came to greet the guests. He was tall and slender, and had a small mustache. There was a merry look in his eyes.

"My, what fun we shall have together," he said to the twins.

Colonel Percy took them in charge at once. While their mother and father accompained Cousin Martha indoors, and a smiling Negro butler carried their bags upstairs, the children went with the plantation owner on a visit to the stables. On the way Flossie amused them all by jumping up and trying to catch the streamers of moss that hung from the tree branches.

"They are almost as curly as your hair, aren't they?" teased Colonel Percy, ruffling the little girl's ringlets.

"The moss-curls must get awful snarls in them, though," replied Flossie gravely. "I wouldn't like to have to comb them out."

"Neither would I," laughed Nan, who often helped comb the tangles from her small sister's hair.

"Are all these stables?" asked Bert as they approached some sprawling white buildings.

"Yes," the colonel replied, "and I love every horse in them." He spoke of the animals as though they were human beings.

"This is Silver Star," said the owner, reaching into a stall which had the upper half of its door open. "He's one of our finest jumpers and isn't afraid of any jump, no matter what the hazard. Are you, you beauty?" he asked, stroking the velvet neck of the thoroughbred.

The beautiful animal whinnied softly and reached down to nuzzle his master's pocket.

"He wants sugar." The colonel laughed and pulled out a lump. "Silver Star has a great sweet tooth."

"Oh, let me give him the sugar, please!" begged Freddie.

"Very well, but be sure you hold it flat in the palm of your hand," said the horse's owner. "I'll lift you up so he won't have so far to reach."

Silver Star gently took the sugar, but Freddie giggled as the animal's soft lips tickled his hand.

"And now," said the colonel, "I have something else to show you," and beckoned to a boy standing near by.

"Jimmy," he said, "these are the Bobbsey Twins. I want you to ride with them while they're at Great Oaks. Please fetch me Topsy and Prince."

"Yes, sir," answered Jimmy and left on a run.

"Who are Prince and Topsy?" asked Bert.

The colonel smiled, putting a friendly hand on the lad's shoulder. "You'll know in a minute."

Then around the corner of the stables came Jimmy, grinning, and leading two darling ponies.

"Oh, aren't they beautiful!" breathed Nan.

"Like them?" asked Colonel Percy, smiling.

"Like them!" cried Nan, bright-eyed. "They're the prettiest little horses I've ever seen. I just love them!"

"Are these Prince and Topsy?" asked Bert, patting the glossy flank of the nearer pony.

The man nodded, enjoying the children's pleasure.

"And they belong to you while you're at Great Oaks," the colonel told them. "There's one condition," he added, as they chorused joyful thanks. "You must take Jimmy with you whenever you ride. As he is your groom, he will be ready to go with you at any time you say."

Now, indeed, the twins were delighted. They had expected to enjoy their stay at Great Oaks. But to be given two lovely ponies of their very own to ride whenever they liked was too wonderful to believe!

"May we go out now?" asked Freddie.

Colonel Percy reminded them that they ought to change their clothes to do this. Since it soon would be suppertime, he suggested that they watch his jumpers being put through their paces.

The little twins refused to be parted from their ponies, however. As they followed their host to the field behind the stables, they asked Jimmy to bring Topsy and Prince along. While the children perched on the fence to watch the jumpers "work out," they kept patting their own little horses.

"Oh, boy, look at that one!" cried Bert suddenly, as an unusually high jump was made by a large brown and white animal.

The twins applauded eagerly, and soon each had his or her "favorite" in the field. Each jump was greeted with groans or cheers, according to the performance of the one selected.

Suddenly one of the horses refused a hazard, skidding to a stop, with feet braced, just as he reached it. The twins gasped as the rider hurtled over the animal's head and landed with a thud on the ground. They were relieved to see the man get to his feet the next minute and say he was not hurt.

"That's Runnymede. He's a bad actor. There's no depending on him," said the colonel, frowning.

"That man doesn't look like an actor to me, and anyway, he hasn't any stage to act on," said Freddie, looking very puzzled.

As they left the place, Colonel Percy explained that the *horse* was the "bad actor," not the *rider*. A "bad actor," he said, was an animal that was tricky and could not be depended upon to do what was expected of him.

"I ought to get rid of Runnymede, but I hate to. I can't help hoping that some day we may make a real jumper of him," he said.

On the way to the house the twins caught a glimpse of long stretches of cultivated fields. The owner said that most of this was corn, although they did grow other vegetables.

"Tomorrow we'll show you the cotton fields," the man told them.

On their way to the house, the twins turned the corner of a bulky stone building. They almost ran into a familiar object. It was the trailer!

"I wonder why it is standing here outside the garage," Flossie mused.

"Prob'bly too big to get inside," Freddie ventured to say.

For some time the Negro workers had been coming in from the fields. One of them, a young man, gave a startled grunt as he came upon the trailer unexpectedly. There was no mistaking his look of fear as his glance traveled from the vehicle to the Bobbseys. His jaw dropped open. With a sudden motion, he turned and made off down the road as fast as he could go!

"Now what is the matter with him?" said Nan wonderingly. "He acted scared to death."

"Probably afraid of the trailer," said Colonel Percy. "I doubt if Rasty ever saw one before."

The children smiled as they went toward the "big house," as the home of the master of Great Oaks was called.

"Colonel Percy, your daughter Susan told us some things were stolen from you," said Nan as they walked along. "Did the police find them?"

"No, they haven't yet," the man replied. "My wife feels bad about it, too. The silver and vases belonged to her grandmother and her Aunt Susan."

"Haven't the police any clues?" asked Bert.

"Not one that I know of. It's very mysterious."

"I'm going to hunt for clues while I'm here," announced Freddie.

The colonel smiled, and asked the little boy if he liked to play detective.

"Why, yes," gasped Freddie. "How did you know?"

By this time the twins had reached the house. They were taken to two bedrooms and introduced to a darling old mammy who looked like someone right out of a story book. Mammy 'Liza, Mrs. Percy said, would serve the children during their visit at Great Oaks.

"Ask Mammy 'Liza for anything you want," their Cousin Martha said with a smile. "Whether it's possible or not, she will do it for you! We all depend on 'Liza here at Great Oaks."

Although Nan and Flossie were delighted with the arrangement, the boys were inclined to be scornful.

"I don't need a nurse!" announced Bert.

"I guess I can get along without anybody to

dress or undress me," said Freddie to his brother in his room, and would not let the woman in!

That evening the kindly old Negress tucked the girls in bed. For a while she fussed about the room, picking up garments, folding them neatly, and laying out fresh clothes for the morning.

"Mammy 'Liza," said Flossie drowsily, "do you know anyone 'round here named Aunt Emma and Uncle Eben? Course they're Dinah's aunt and uncle, not ours," she added.

"There's a couple o' sharecroppers near here called Emma and Eben. Reckon they're the ones you mean," said the old woman.

"What's a—a—sharecropper?" asked Flossie, half asleep.

"A sharecropper, honey, is a planter that raises cotton on land he rents from the owner, with tools the owner lends him. When the crop's ripe, he shares it with the owner. That's how come he's called a sharecropper."

The girls were hardly aware that Mammy 'Liza had put out their light and was stealing softly from the room. The next thing they knew, a bell somewhere outside the house was ringing loudly. The boys were awakened by it, too.

"It's a fire!" cried Freddie. "Come on!"

He was so excited that he did not wait to put on bathrobe or slippers. In his bare feet and pajamas he raced down the stairs as fast as his chubby legs would carry him.

CHAPTER XVI

THE LAND OF COTTON

DOWN the stairs, through the hall, and onto the porch ran Freddie. Then he stopped to listen again for the bell. The sound seemed to come from across the road, so up the driveway he went.

"Well, well, son," said a voice as he reached the entrance, "where are you going?"

The little boy looked up to see a tall man blocking his path. Colonel Percy!

"Where's the fire?" cried Freddie excitedly.

"Fire? There's no fire," replied the plantation owner, smiling.

Poor Freddie! He suddenly realized how funny he must look, out so early in the morning in pajamas and bare feet, looking for something that wasn't!

"But the bell. What's that for?" he asked.

"It's to call the workers," answered Colonel Percy. "Some of them have to go so far to pick cotton that they ride out in wagons and trucks. You run back to the house and get your clothes on. Then I'll take you to see them."

Freddie found Nan and Flossie up. He told them to dress quickly and follow him. As Mammy 'Liza had laid out their play dresses, the girls were ready first. Bert and Freddie were a little sorry they had not let her help them, for they always disliked having the girls get ahead of them!

Colonel Percy was waiting for the children. He drove them in a car to watch the wagons and trucks being loaded with cotton pickers. The Negroes, both men and women, were gaily dressed in bright-colored shirts, or sunbonnets and aprons. Most of them were singing.

"They must like their work," said Nan. "They seem so happy."

"Cotton picking is healthful exercise." The plantation owner smiled.

He said no more, but the children knew the workers were happy because they liked Colonel Percy.

"After breakfast we'll go see them in the fields," he said. "It will be very sunny, so put on hats. Now I must attend to several things. Wouldn't you twins like to go for a ride on your ponies?"

Would they! As fast as they could, they ran toward the stables. Out of breath they said good morning to Jimmy, to Prince and to Topsy. Their young groom greeted them with the same wide-mouthed grin he had worn the day before.

"You all be ridin' today?" he questioned shyly.

"We'd like to go now," said Bert, as Nan stroked Topsy's soft nose.

"They're good little ponies and sure do like to be exercised!" replied Jimmy. "I'll go get the saddles."

It was decided that the boys should go out first with the Negro lad. The ponies walked slowly until their riders got used to them. Then they went a little faster.

"I can hardly wait," cried Flossie, peeking through a rail fence at her brothers, who were going around the small riding ring. "Ooh —Freddie nearly fell off!"

"Jimmy caught him just in time!" Nan sighed in relief.

The young groom certainly understood little boys as well as horses. He seemed to have known Freddie was going to try a gallop!

Nan and Flossie did not ride very long, for Mammy 'Liza came to tell them breakfast was ready. "You children got up with the sun, sure 'nough," she laughed.

At the table Mr. Bobbsey said he had spoken to Mr. Hopper, the owner of the trailer, on the telephone. The man planned to drive over to get his property.

"And what do you think?" the twins' father added. "He's going to take me to a very old place near here where a house and a barn are being torn down. In it are good old pine boards that I believe will match some of the samples I have with me."

Everyone was pleased, for they knew Daddy Bobbsey would have been sorry if he had not found enough old lumber to make his trip worth while.

"I'm going to work, too, this morning," said Freddie. "I have to pick cotton."

Gaily the twins got ready for their trip to the fields. Nan and Flossie tied on the sunbonnets which they had brought on the journey. Mammy 'Liza brought out two aprons with a large front pocket in each to hold cotton. Even the smaller apron was too large for Flossie, and they had a good deal of fun trying to pin it up so that the little twin would not trip over it.

When the girls joined Bert and Freddie outside, they found that the boys had on large straw hats. Gunnysacks were thrown over their shoulders to put their cotton pickings in.

As they were about to start, a foreman stepped up to Colonel Percy. One of the pickers had failed to report for work that morning, he said. He found the fellow had left the plantation.

"It's that man Rasty, suh," he added. "He's been actin' pow'ful queer lately, anyway. This mornin' he ain't showed up at all. We're shorthanded, too."

"Well, do the best you can, and I'll give Rasty a talking-to when I see him," Colonel Percy promised.

As they started for the cotton fields in a car, the older twins tried to recall where they had heard the name Rasty before.

"Oh, I know," said Nan. "He's the one who was afraid of the trailer yesterday."

"Maybe he's still 'fraid of it and doesn't dare to come back to Great Oaks," Freddie suggested.

"That won't bother him much longer. The trailer will be gone soon," Bert pointed out.

"Well, in any case it doesn't make much difference. Rasty is kind of slow at his work," the colonel said.

The children could not dismiss the matter so easily. Rasty had aroused their curiosity and they could not help but feel there was something mysterious about him. As they came in sight of the cotton fields, however, they forgot all about him.

For here, at last, they had come face to face with King Cotton in all his glory. As far as the eye could see, there was field after field of the magic plant. It was like a great green carpet, thickly sprinkled with white over the top where the cotton bolls had burst open, exposing the fluffy lint within. All over the fields men and women were at work picking.

The children hoped to start their task at once, but Colonel Percy said he first wanted to show them how the cotton grew.

"The seeds are planted in January," he said. "Then when the plants grow up, lovely yellow flowers appear. From these come the bolls which later burst open."

"And the white cotton is inside!" finished Flossie.

"That's right," replied the colonel. "A long, long time ago someone in India discovered cotton. He wrote down, 'The plant has fruit, within which there is a lamb. This has fleece of great beauty.' "

Flossie's eyes were big as she said, "But it wasn't a lamb at all, was it?"

"No, it was only the lint as you see it here." The plantation owner laughed, stooping to pick a tuft of the fluffy stuff.

"But it feels almost like a lamb," said Freddie, stroking the soft lint thoughtfully. "It's so soft."

"How many months do you pick cotton?" asked Bert.

"Until Christmas, if the weather is good," the man replied. "If we need a little decoration for our tree, we can—"

Suddenly Flossie gave a frightened scream. She began dancing about among the cotton plants, flapping her large apron and wailing:

"Something ran up my leg! Oh! Oh-h dear! I think it's a mouse!"

The little girl was so scared that it was some time before anyone could quiet her long enough to help her.

"Stand still, Flossie!" Nan ordered. "How do you suppose—"

The sentence was never finished. Just then the mouse fell to the ground and scurried off among the plants. Colonel Percy and the boys searched for some time, hoping to find its nest. But they did not see it.

"Now we'd better start the game of picking cotton," the plantation owner said, showing the Bobbsey children just how to do it. "A prize to the one who gets the most."

It was great fun. Although the sun was hot and their backs grew tired from stooping over so long, the twins stuck to their task. After a while the boys had their gunnysacks filled and the girls' aprons were so full that lint peeked from the tops of them. The colonel praised them, and suggested weighing the cotton at the gin to see who would win the prize.

"But actually, I think each of you deserves a reward," he smiled.

On the way Bert wanted to know why it was called a gin. "It's kind of a queer name," he said.

The colonel explained that "gin" really was only a short way of saying "engine." This was a nickname the Negroes had given the machine which separated the lint from the seeds and dust to make pure white cotton.

"Now we also call the building the machine is in a gin," he said.

After weighing their pickings, the colonel said he guessed Bert really had won the prize. Then he showed the children exactly what the gin machine did.

"Do they use the cotton seed for anything except planting?" Nan asked.

"Yes, indeed," replied their host, smiling at her. "Cotton seed is full of oil. This can be used in food—as in salad dressing—or used on machinery."

On the way home Colonel Percy told them that the chief thing they had to fear in the gin was fire. If allowed to gain headway, the flames could wipe out valuable stock in short time.

Freddie looked worried. "I wish Daddy had let me bring my fire engine," he said.

Then his thoughts were turned to something more pleasant by the arrival of their young cousin, Susan Percy. Nan wanted to hear all about the wedding at which she had been a bridesmaid.

Bert was up early the next morning and went for a brisk ride on Prince. On his way back to the house, he paused to watch an old Negro with white wooly hair. The man was clipping a boxwood hedge, and groaning as he did so.

"I got a misery in my back," the old fellow explained. "And that worthless Rasty has to turn up missin' today!"

"Rasty?" asked Bert. "You mean the one who ran away? I thought he worked in the cotton fields."

"He does, son," replied the gardener, "but one day a week he's supposed to help me around the big house here. Oh, my back!" he groaned as he stooped to pick up some of the green clippings.

"Maybe I can pitch in," Bert offered. "I work in the garden at home sometimes."

The old man looked surprised, but grateful.

"Well, it'd be right helpful," he said. "If you want to bring me that old wheelbarrow—"

"Sure, I'll get it. Be back in a minute," said Bert, dashing off.

The lad had just picked up the handles of the wheelbarrow when he saw something white stuck in a crack of the wood. It was a slip of

paper, which Bert quickly pulled out. There was something written on the sheet that made him suddenly stiffen in surprise.

"Jumping crickets!" Bert exclaimed. "Wait till everybody sees this!"

Quickly setting down the wheelbarrow, he raced into the house.

CHAPTER XVII

THE BALKY RADIO

THE first person Bert saw at the house was the one he most wanted to see. That was Mrs. Martha Percy.

"Look!" he cried excitedly. "I've got it. I've found a clue to the robbery! It's a real clue this time."

He thrust the slip of paper into Mrs. Percy's hand. She regarded it with sharp interest.

"Why, this looks like—it *is*—a list of the things that were stolen from us! Where did you find it?" she asked quickly.

It took Bert only a moment to tell the story. He had just finished when Nan appeared and had to be told.

"Oh, Bert, what do you make of it?" the girl cried. "Who could have put that paper in the wheelbarrow?"

"The thief, of course."

"Why would he put it in an old dirty wheelbarrow?" the girl asked.

Her twin had an idea. "If the wheelbarrow was full of dirt, it would make a swell hiding place for pieces of silver. The thief stuck the list in a crack of the wood and forgot it."

Mrs. Percy looked at the Bobbsey boy admiringly. "My dear, that is a very clever thought," she said. "We've always felt it was strange that our hunting dogs didn't bark when the thief was here. This might prove that someone on the plantation took the things."

"How about the old man out there clipping the boxwood?" asked Bert. "But he looks so honest."

"He is," replied Mrs. Percy. "Old Nebo wouldn't take a thing."

"How about Rasty?" inquired the boy. "He is supposed to help Nebo."

The mistress of Great Oaks plantation looked startled. "He could have been the thief," she said slowly, "for he worked in the house once in a while as well as in the garden. He would know what we own."

"Is that his writing on the paper?" asked Nan eagerly.

"I really don't know," Mrs. Percy replied. "I'll ask the cook."

The twins went with her to the kitchen. To their disappointment they were told the handwriting was not that of Rasty. The cook showed them a Christmas card with the young Negro's signature on it.

"There goes my clue," said Bert with a sigh.

"But somebody wrote it, so it's still a valuable clue," Nan defended her twin.

"I shall turn the paper over to the sheriff," said Mrs. Percy. "I'll drive to his office this morning."

Her husband had gone to town on business, so it was not until later in the day that he was able to talk over the important find with Nan and Bert. By that time they had some new ideas to offer.

"Maybe the real thief used Rasty to take the heirlooms out of your house," said the boy.

"He put them in the wheelbarrow under some dirt, and wheeled them to the thief's car," added Nan. "That's why the dogs didn't bark."

"I can't see why Rasty didn't run away before," said the colonel. "He didn't seem to be scared until you people came."

Suddenly Bert shouted, "Why didn't I think of that before? He wasn't afraid of *us*. He was afraid of the trailer!"

Colonel Percy and Nan caught the boy's meaning at the same time. "You think the man who took the trailer stole the old silver and vases, too. At least, he got Rasty to do it for him."

"Yes," replied the Bobbsey lad excitedly. "He wrote on the paper the things he wanted."

"The sheriff did find tire tracks on a lane that's usually used only by horses and mules," said Colonel Percy. "I'll telephone to him right away and ask him to compare the impression in the road with the tread on the tires of the trailer."

"Hasn't it rained since he looked at them?" asked Nan. "How could he see the marks in the lane now?"

"Oh, he took photographs of them when he first saw them," the plantation owner replied.

Upon hearing the story, the sheriff said he would go at once to Mr. Hopper's house to take pictures of the treads on the trailer tires.

"As soon as they are developed, I'll bring them over to Great Oaks," the officer promised.

The twins hoped this would happen the next morning, but they were to be disappointed. They forgot it for the time being, as a special trip had been planned for all the Bobbsey children.

Mammy 'Liza had mentioned to them that Uncle Eben had been up to the colonel's gin with a "passel" of cotton. This had made the twins realize that they had put off their visit to see him and Aunt Emma long enough. They still had the radio which Dinah had asked them to present to her relatives!

Their Cousin Susan, learning of this, had said she would drive them to the sharecroppers' cabin. It was a lovely day and they set out happily.

"We'll take the river road. It's a longer way 'round," said Susan, "but I think you will like it better. The levees are interesting, too, in case you've never seen any."

"What are levees?" Freddie asked.

"They are what people build along the bank

of a river to hold back the water when there's a flood," their cousin explained. "Men used to pile up earth, stones or sandbags, but nowadays a good many levees are made of cement. I'll show them to you as we drive along."

The river road was really very beautiful. The water itself looked so peaceful and calm that it was hard to believe it ever could rise and run over the land.

"Sometimes even the levees can't hold back a flood altogether," Susan said. "Then the water does all sorts of damage. Sometimes it even carries away small houses."

"Golly, I wouldn't like that very much," said Freddie.

When they had gone about a mile, the main road left the river. Susan now drove along a narrow dirt lane near the water's edge. Here and there were shacks. Bright-eyed Negro children waved to the Bobbseys as they passed.

"If it's dangerous to live here, why do people have their places so close to the river?" asked Bert.

"Because the soil is very rich," replied his cousin. "The water brings with it a good deal of rich dirt and this is washed up over the land. You can grow just about anything in it. Look, children, there's Aunt Emma and Uncle Eben's cabin."

Just ahead was an unpainted wooden shack with a chimney in the center of the peaked roof. A small porch sagged on one side, but this was hardly noticeable because a trumpet vine almost covered it.

"I wonder if Aunt Emma and Uncle Eben are home," said Flossie as she went up the steps.

"Yes, they are," said Susan. She opened a screen door and called cheerfully, "Aunt Emma, Uncle Eben, where are you?"

"Well, bless my soul, if it isn't Miss Susan! You're sure 'nough welcome, my honey. Come in, come on in!"

If the voice was pleasant, the owner of it was even more so. Dinah's Aunt Emma was a small woman. Her face was criss-crossed with wrinkles that made it seem as if she were smiling all the time.

Behind her stood a tall man with fuzzy white hair. This was Uncle Eben. He hustled about, setting out chairs for the callers, while Susan explained about the Bobbsey twins and their reason for coming to see their cook's relative.

"Well, this is sure a surprise," cried Aunt Emma, beaming at the twins. "So our niece Dinah hasn't forgotten us!" She busied herself putting a kettle of water on the stove to boil.

"Oh, no, she talks of you a lot," said Flossie, "and she sent you and Uncle Eben a present."

Bert set the portable radio on the table before the two old people.

"Is it one of those things that talks and plays music?" Uncle Eben asked excitedly. "Can we hear it now?" He stroked the radio top with trembling fingers.

"Oh, yes," said Nan. She turned the knobs and faint music came to them; another turn and an advertisement for soap!

It was clear that the old people did not care what program was on. They were more interested in the fact that sounds were coming from the box!

"Well, I declare to goodness," said Uncle Eben.

"Don't that beat all!" cried Aunt Emma.

She was so fascinated by the wonderful new toy that she was startled when the tea kettle on the stove boiled over with a hissing noise. Aunt Emma made tea for Susan Percy, and Uncle Eben poured delicious homemade root beer for the children. They also had some of Aunt Emma's cookies and good strawberry jam. While the callers ate, both old people asked them many questions about Dinah and Sam.

As the children were about to leave, Susan asked the old people if they knew Rasty, who worked on the plantation and had run away.

"Yes, and he's a no'count, shiftless boy," said Uncle Eben. "No one ever knows what Rasty's going to be up to next."

"Will you let us know if you see him?" the twins' cousin asked.

"I'll keep an eye out for that rascal," promised Uncle Eben.

Just before they left, Aunt Emma asked Bert to show her how to run the radio.

"Why, sure, it's easy. Look here," said Bert.

He turned the knobs but not a sound came forth! The radio was dead!

No amount of tinkering would fix it. Finally Bert said he would have to take the portable into town to be repaired.

"Reckon it won't take too long, will it?" asked Uncle Eben wistfully.

Bert promised to bring the radio back to them as good as new in a few days. Then the callers left.

"We'll take the woods road," she said, as she slipped behind the steering wheel of her car and started the motor. "There's a small stream with the prettiest little white covered bridge over it you ever saw."

"Is it the kind where you pay to go across?" asked Nan.

"It used to be," replied her cousin. "Now it's free. About a mile beyond that we'll put the car on a flat-bottomed boat and go to the other side of the river."

"That will be fun," cried Freddie. Then as they came to the white bridge, he added, "I want to get out and walk across. I never walked on a bridge with a roof over it."

Bert and Freddie got out of the automobile and trotted ahead of it. They reached the far bank of the stream when the automobile was only halfway across.

"Let's hide in the woods, Bert," suggested Freddie, "and make Nan and Flossie hunt for us!"

"All right," agreed his brother, starting forward.

At this point the woods were dense with tall trees and underbrush. The Bobbsey boys had not gone far, when suddenly a snarling animal dropped from a tree directly ahead of them.

Freddie screamed, then backed away.

CHAPTER XVIII

TELLTALE PHOTOGRAPHS

WHEN Susan Percy heard Freddie scream, she forgot all about the speed law. Quickly she drove the car the rest of the way across the covered bridge and hopped out.

"Where are you?" she called, as Nan and Flossie jumped from the automobile.

What a sight met their eyes! A huge bobcat crouched near the two boys.

"Oh!" screamed Flossie. "Don't let it hurt them!"

Bert had put his little brother behind him and reached for a big stick. Susan rushed forward, calling: "Scat! Scat!"

Suddenly there came the sharp baying of hounds. In a moment two hunting dogs burst from the thicket and charged the wildcat. It sprang to the trunk of a fallen tree and stood there, spitting and snarling at the other two animals.

Quickly Bert and Freddie ran toward the car. They would leave the battle of the forest to take care of itself! After they were safe, Flossie began to feel sorry for the beautiful bobcat.

"Oh, the poor kitty!" she said, as Susan drove off. "Those horrid dogs will kill it, won't they?"

"Don't you worry, that cat will take care of itself!" replied her cousin. "The hounds are afraid of it, really. They'll worry the pussy a little for the fun of the thing, and then they'll go home."

As they rode along, she told the children more about the boat they were going to ride on.

"It has no engines or oars or paddles," she said.

"Then how does it go?" asked Freddie.

"A man with a long, heavy pole shoves it through the water. The stream isn't very deep. In fact," laughed Susan, "it's more like a mud river with a little water on top of it!"

Freddie said he hoped it wasn't like a bog, and told his cousin how he had nearly been sucked under the mud at Tinky's home.

"This isn't dangerous," Susan assured him, "but I shouldn't advise you to fall in just the same!"

Presently they came to the ferry crossing. There stood a smiling man waiting for passengers. His flat-bottomed boat was just big enough to hold one automobile. After Susan drove on, the man put up the wooden flaps at the ends of his river ferry and unfastened the chain which held the craft to a tree stump.

"All aboard!" he laughed, as he stuck a long pole into the shore and pushed off.

The way he made the boat go was really with his feet. He stood at the front of it, facing the rear, and stuck his pole firmly into the mud. Holding tightly to it, he started to step.

"He's walking standing still!" cried Flossie as the craft began to move.

When the back end of the ferry reached the man, he lifted up the pole, walked to the front end of the boat, and started his work all over again.

"I'd like to help him," said Bert.

Susan let the lad get out of the car, but asked the others to stay inside. The boy tried to pole the boat, but he could not make it go an inch!

"Guess you'll have to get a little stronger, son, before you can do such heavy work," said the ferryman.

"I didn't know it was so hard."

Inside the automobile Freddie was calling attention to a wire which was strung overhead from a big tree on one side of the river to another on the far bank. From this there hung another wire attached to their boat.

"That's to keep this flat we're on from going down the river," said Susan. "When the water runs very swiftly, or the wind blows hard, a man wouldn't be able to keep the boat from going downstream."

"Wouldn't it be fun to be lost in a car on a river?" giggled Flossie.

"I don't think so," replied Nan seriously.

"These rivers around here can play bad tricks during storms," added her cousin.

Soon the ferry reached the bank, and the man let Bert fasten the chain. The boy thought that he was doing exactly as he was directed. But alas! Something went wrong. As Susan started her motor and drove off the flat, only the front wheels got away. The chain came loose, the boat slipped into the river, and the rear wheels of the car sank in the soft earth.

"Oh, oh!" cried Nan. "What shall we do now?"

Susan was very calm, but it was plain that she was worried. She got out and looked the situation over.

"I'm terribly sorry," said Bert. "I'll shove the back of the car while you run the engine."

Susan tried this, and the ferryman helped push the car. But it was no use. The rear wheels spun round and round, but did not move.

"I guess we'll have to walk to town and get help," sighed Susan.

"Let me go," offered Bert. "This was all my fault."

The poor boy was red-faced and puffing. He was spattered with black mud from head to feet!

"You'd scare the people in town, the way you look," said Freddie.

Before a decision could be made, a car appeared on the road ahead. It came straight toward them.

"Oh, maybe this man will pull us out," said Nan.

The stranger proved to be kind and helpful. He took a tow rope from his automobile and handed it to the ferryman.

"Hitch these folks' car to mine," he directed. "I'll have 'em out on the road in a jiffy."

In another moment the two cars were bound together and then a real "tug-of-war" began. Blocks of wood were put behind the rear wheels of Susan's car. The stranger, pulling as hard as he dared, was able to move the Percy car inch by inch. Finally it stood on firm ground.

"Oh, thank you so much," said Susan warmly. "I don't know what we would have done without you!"

"We ought to give him a prize," said Flossie.

"You mean a reward," corrected Nan.

"He wouldn't take anything," said Susan. "People often get stuck with their cars around here. We're glad to help out one another."

"Well, couldn't I just give him one tiny cookie that Aunt Emma made?" pleaded Flossie. "Maybe he's hungry."

Susan laughed. "All right, go ahead."

The stranger accepted the cookie with a smile. He patted Flossie's shoulder and said he wished he had a little girl with golden curls just like hers. The Bobbseys watched him drive his car onto the boat which the ferryman had pulled to the shore. Then they waved good-bye and left.

"This has been a wonderful day," said Nan when they reached Great Oaks.

She thought the excitement was over, but she was mistaken. The Bobbsey Twins were greeted by Mammy 'Liza who held out two letters to them, one for Nan, the other for Bert.

"Oh, mine's from Nellie Parks!" cried the girl, tearing open the envelope.

She looked at it quickly, then said she would read the message aloud. It went:

"Dear Nan,

We hope you are having a good time. We miss you all very much. When are you coming home?

Grace Lavine and I and one of Bert's friends decided to form a club. It is called the Find Waggo Club. Every day we take turns hunting for him. I am the president and I am sorry to report that we haven't found him yet.

Dinah sends her love to you—and Snap and Snoop. Your cat caught a mouse yesterday.

With love,

NELLIE."

"Gee, that's nice of them to form the club," said Bert.

"But I'm 'fraid we'll never see Waggo any more," sighed Flossie.

Bert's letter proved to be more satisfying. It was from Tinky and gave some real information. The trailer, he said, had contained several boxes and barrels when he stowed away in it. The boxes, he added, were sealed, and he had no idea what was in them. They had been taken out in Lakeport. Tinky had not thought to mention these things, as he had no idea they had been stolen.

"Here's a clue, though," said Bert, reading the letter again. "Tinky says he remembers that one box had a name on it."

"Does he give the address too?" Nan asked.

"Yes," said Bert, reading on a little way. "The name was R. Beever and the address was New York. I don't suppose that helps us very much, really," he added, looking up. "There must be a lot of people named Beever in New York."

"Maybe not. Anyway, we ought to tell the police," insisted Nan.

Colonel Percy was much interested in Tinky's letter and asked Bert to show it to the sheriff.

"He's coming to Great Oaks tonight with the photographs of the trailer tires," he said.

The small twins were very tired and went to bed soon after dinner. For once they did not mind, since they wanted to wake up very early.

About nine o'clock that night the sheriff arrived. The Percys and Bobbseys were eager to hear his report.

"I have news that may be good," he said, after the usual greetings. He smiled at Nan and Bert and wagged his finger at them playfully. "You youngsters are pretty smart," he went on, "and I don't mind saying you've helped me a lot. Take these tire prints now."

He unwound a strip of paper and placed the palms of his hands flat on the corners to hold it down on top of a table. The twins gathered around him excitedly, while the men looked over their shoulders.

"You see, here are the marks of the tires we found on your back lane right after the robbery," he said to the colonel.

"Now these," he went on, unrolling a second strip of photographs and placing it near the first, "are pictures we have just taken of the tire prints of Mr. Hopper's trailer, the one you Bobbsey Twins found in Lakeport."

"Why, the two sets of marks look just alike!" cried Nan and Bert together.

"I said you children are smart," said the sheriff admiringly. "Yes, sir, I believe they *are* the same. Of course, I'm not sayin' it's so, but it does look as if Mr. Hopper's trailer was in your back road, Colonel, on the night of the theft."

"Then the trailer *did* have something to do with the robbery!" said Nan.

"It begins to look like it, miss," said the sheriff. "Now if we could just catch that man Rasty," he added thoughtfully.

Susan now told of finding out where Rasty's people lived, and of how Aunt Emma and Uncle Eben had promised to let her know if they should see him.

"I'd like to show you a letter," said Bert to the officer, telling him who Tinky was and how he happened to be connected with the trailer mystery.

"Well, well," said the sheriff, "this is a clue, indeed. You children certainly are putting the police on their toes," he laughed.

With the statement that he would get in touch with the New York authorities at once, the man left. On their way up to bed, the twins talked over the latest angles of the mystery.

"It's a little nearer being solved," said Nan as she opened the door to her bedroom and bade her brother good night.

Early the next morning the Bobbsey Twins were awakened by Mammy 'Liza. The good old nurse helped Nan and Flossie into bathrobe and slippers and drew them to the window.

"Look down there," she directed, pointing to the driveway.

Below them was a line of men and women on horseback. A red-coated figure sat at the head of the procession. Colonel Percy's hounds milled about him, yelping.

"Reckon you never saw anything like that before!" said Mammy 'Liza proudly. "They're ready for the hunt."

CHAPTER XIX

THE HUNT BREAKFAST

"READY for the hunt!" repeated Flossie, hopping about excitedly. "Oh, Mammy 'Liza, hurry and get us dressed! We're going on the hunt, too!"

"No, honey," said the old nurse soothingly. "You're only going to the hunt breakfast and you've plenty of time before that."

"The breakfast comes *after* the fox hunt?" Nan asked.

"That's right. I reckon the folks want to work up a good appetite," the old woman said.

Suddenly the man in the bright coat lifted a horn to his lips and blew a musical blast. As though this were a signal, the excited dogs raced away, the red-coated leader and the others in full pursuit.

"They're off!" Nan cried, wide-eyed. "We'll have to hurry, or we won't get to the breakfast on time."

But Mammy 'Liza had a surprise for them. From a trunk she brought out four beautiful riding costumes which, she said, had belonged to Susan and her brother.

Joyfully the twins dressed themselves.

"You look bee-yoo-ti-ful, Nan," said Flossie as the girls left their room.

"Thank you, dear." Her sister smiled.

When they reached the stables, the children found Jimmy waiting. He was to ride with them to the hunt breakfast. He had saddled Prince and Topsy for the younger twins and had brought two extra ponies for Nan and Bert.

It was a long ride through beautiful woods to the picnic spot, and the children did not hurry, as Jimmy assured them the hunters always took longer than they expected to run the fox to earth.

"I hear them!" cried Freddie suddenly.

Just then the children rode into a clearing and saw ahead of them an attractive hunting lodge. Tables for breakfast has been set out in the open. Around them gathered the hunters.

There was Susan, too, near a group of girls and young men. She was the first to spy the twins, as they cantered into the clearing.

"How darling you all look!" she cried.

Soon the waiters appeared from the lodge with steaming dishes, and there was a general movement toward the tables. A few moments later the twins found themselves seated between Mother and Daddy Bobbsey with bowls of peppery stew before them. Freddie took one mouthful of the food. He choked, and had to be patted on the back.

"It's too hot," he sputtered. "It b-burns my throat!"

The other children, not used to such highly

seasoned food, felt the same way as Freddie did. Though they would have tried to eat it to be polite, they were very much relieved when something else was brought to them. Mammy 'Liza had sent over some cereal and cream for their special use!

"She thinks of just everything," said Flossie, as she put her spoon into the bowl of familiar food.

After breakfast the twins rode back to the house with Colonel Percy. He asked them if they would like to go into town to see an auction.

"You may ride farm style with Mammy 'Liza and Jimmy, if you like," he said.

When the twins learned that the trip was to be made in an open wagon drawn by two of the plantation mules, they laughed.

"I hope they won't sit down and refuse to go," said Nan, and told the man about the mule Jonathan who would not work when strangers were around.

The twins started upstairs to change their clothes, but Susan stopped them to snap their pictures in the hunting costumes. Then with Mammy's help the girls put on play suits, beating the boys downstairs by five minutes.

Jimmy was ready, so the Bobbsey Twins and the old nurse climbed aboard the farm cart with shouts of glee. The driver clucked to the animals and off they went, the creaky wagon bumping along the road. It was a slow ride and not a very comfortable one, but the twins enjoyed it, even though Flossie nearly bit her tongue trying to say:

"Th-this is a j-jouncy ride!"

"Never mind, honey, you'll be coming back in a car," replied Mammy.

Then the children learned that both the mules and the cart were to be sold at the auction. Colonel Percy would drive to town to pick up the twins and the servants.

When they reached the village, Freddie pointed. "Is that where they sell things?" he asked.

He was looking toward the market square, where a throng of people had gathered. A man stood up on a box with a stand in front of him. Every once in a while he would hit the top of the stand with a wooden hammer.

"La-deez and gentlemen—" they could hear him say. "I'm bid one dollar, two dollars. Any more?"

"He's the auctioneer," said Bert to the little twins. "And look at all the things he has to sell!"

It seemed to the twins that almost every sort of thing came to the auctioneer's block. Farm tools, bags of grain, seed, shawls, blankets, furniture, and animals. One of these was a wild-eyed nanny goat which Freddie fell in love with and wanted to take back with them to Great Oaks!

"He'd butt you right off the place!" laughed Mammy 'Liza.

At last came the time for the mules from Great Oaks to be sold. The twins and Mammy got out of the wagon, while Jimmy drove it around the auctioneer's block so everyone could see it. The crowd was not interested. In fact, the bidding was so slow that the little twins decided to take a hand and help things along.

They climbed onto the platform. Freddie held up his hand for silence, as he had seen the auctioneer do.

"Ladies and gentlemen," he cried shrilly, "your attention, plee—eeze!"

The tone was almost exactly like the auctioneer's, except in a high pitch, and everyone turned to look.

"These mu-els are very good mu-els!" continued Freddie. "They b'long to Colonel Percy, and you know him!"

Cheers arose from the crowd, mingled with friendly laughter.

"Flossie, say something," whispered Freddie. "I can't think of anything else!"

"The mules are gentle and nice," shouted the little girl. "They won't ever run away."

"And they can pull any load, even two sets of twins!" finished Freddie.

Everyone laughed at this, for word had been passed around who the Northern children were. Good-naturedly the crowd began to bid. When it was over, both mules and wagon had been sold to a farmer at a fancy price—much more than the colonel had expected to get for them.

"Oh, there's the sheriff!" cried Bert suddenly. "I'm going to ask him if he has found out anything about the trailer thief."

The boy dashed off. While waiting for him, the other children looked at things people had to sell which had not been in the auction. One shy old lady had something in a basket. When Nan and Flossie saw what was inside, they made up their minds to buy the contents at once, and give them as a present to Cousin Martha, whose birthday it was.

Bert returned just as Colonel Percy drove up. The lad told them that the sheriff had just found out a silver platter belonging to the Percys had been located at R. Beever's in New York.

"So Tinky's clue was a good one," said Nan.

"They haven't found the thief, though," Bert went on. "They don't even know his real name yet."

Colonel Percy and the Bobbsey Twins discussed the mystery all the way to the plantation. This ride was quite different from the trip into town and the children were home before they knew it.

"We'll have to dress for Cousin Martha's birthday dinner," said Nan as she and Flossie went to their room an hour later.

The two girls looked very sweet when they appeared a little while later. Nan had on a crisp organdy frock, and Flossie was like a little fairy in a soft blue dress.

Susan, as pretty as a picture, met them at the

foot of the stairs. "Everything is ready," she whispered.

"We'll go to the dining room now," said Mrs. Percy.

At the door she paused, amazed, while the twins cried out:

"Surprise, surprise!"

"Why, how lovely! Did you dear children take all this trouble just for me?" cried Mrs. Percy.

The dining room looked like a flower garden. With the servants' help, the children and Susan had decorated it with greens and flowers from the garden. In the center of the table was a large bouquet, around which were candles in lovely silver holders—Susan's special gift to her mother.

"Goodness, I believe there never was a woman as fortunate as I am," said the good lady, as she opened package after package.

She was delighted with the gold and black vase from Mr. and Mrs. Bobbsey. Besides the candlesticks, there were the other gifts of silver from Colonel Percy. Last of all, Mrs. Percy lifted a present which had an odd wording on the top.

" 'Twins from the Twins,' " she read. "Now I wonder what this can be!"

CHAPTER XX

THE RIVER BOAT

NAN AND BERT looked eagerly at their Cousin Martha, and the little twins squirmed in their chairs.

"Open it!" begged Flossie.

"You're going to be surprised," added Freddie.

To tease them, Mrs. Percy took a long time to untie the ribbon. Then she pretended to look at the bottom of the box and even shook it a little to try guessing what was inside. Just when the Bobbsey children were sure they could wait no longer, the woman opened her present.

"Well, I declare to goodness!" she cried.

"What is it, Mother?" asked Susan, who had not been told the secret.

"This is just too sweet for words. Two baby turkeys and they're exactly alike."

"That's why we bought them when we were at the auction, 'cause they're twins," said Flossie, clapping her hands. "And *we're* twins, so that's why we wrote what we did on the box."

" 'Twins from the Twins,' " Cousin Martha

read again. "That was a lovely thought of yours. This gift is almost," she added, smiling at the children, "the nicest present of all!"

During the meal there was much joking, and the Bobbsey Twins kept their elders amused with stories of their recent adventures.

"I got pretty red in the face when the radio Dinah sent down to her Aunt Emma wouldn't work," said Bert. "I'd like to take it to town to get it fixed, and bring it back very soon."

"Suppose you do so tomorrow," suggested Colonel Percy. "A cotton barge is going down the river from here. You children would enjoy a ride with the captain. He's a fine old man. While the cotton is being unloaded in town to be put on freight cars, you might skip up to a store, Bert, with your radio."

"Thank you, sir," replied the boy. "That will be a good chance to get it fixed."

When the children reached the Great Oaks wharf the next morning, Negroes already were at work carrying bales of cotton onto the barge.

"It looks like a giant flat-bottomed boat," said Freddie. "Only of course it's a little higher out of the water."

"Look there." The colonel pointed to a packet boat coming upstream with a captain aboard. "That's going to push the barge."

"Up North we'd call it a tugboat," said Bert.

"That's right." The plantation owner smiled. "Long ago a good deal of the mail around here was carried by these small steamboats. Since they brought letters and packages, they were called packet boats. The name has stuck, although most of their work now is pushing barges."

The children met Captain Smith, who said he would gladly take them to town and back. He even said Bert and Freddie might perch themselves on top of the bales of cotton, if they would sit very still and stay near the two men who would be on board.

"We'll wave to you from our boat," said Flossie.

The girls went up to the little tower where the captain steered the boat. It was fun watching the scenes along the shores. Suddenly Flossie, looking ahead, screamed.

"Oo, Freddie's falling!" she cried.

The little boy had grown tired of sitting still, and had jumped from one pile of cotton to another. He had misstepped and now was rolling down, loosening bales as he went.

"Hi! Sailor!" shouted the captain.

Just in time one of the men on the barge turned and caught Freddie up. But two bales of cotton went into the water!

The little boy promised to sit in one place. This was not hard work now, for several Negroes on the packet began to sing and dance.

One of them brought out a guitar. To his strumming some of the others sang, while two young fellows started to shuffle in their bare feet, grinning all the while. They were good dancers. The twins clapped delightedly as the lads did an old-fashioned "buck and wing."

"They ought to be on the stage," exclaimed Nan.

The show kept up until the town wharf was reached, then the dancers had to unload the cotton. Since the boat would dock for an hour before returning, the children decided to go ashore and see the sights. Bert had Aunt Emma's radio with him.

A shop near the dock promised to have the radio repaired in plenty of time. The boy thanked the proprietor and joined his brother and sisters outside. The town was a quaint place, full of friendly people.

"Let's buy a few souvenirs to give to our chums in Lakeport," suggested Nan.

"We ought to get something for each member of the Find Waggo Club," added Bert.

For three-quarters of an hour the Bobbseys were busy, selecting toys and other articles made of cotton, pine and sugar cane.

"Nellie Parks loves molasses taffy," said Nan. "I'm going to take her a box of it."

"And my friend Susie Larker just 'dores jewelry," spoke up Flossie. "She'll like this banjo pin."

With only ten minutes of the hour left, Bert reminded them they must return to the wharf. He started ahead to pick up the radio, and the others followed.

All the way back to Great Oaks, as they sailed along, they played a game of seeing which child could name the most articles made of cotton—ticles made of cotton—or partly made of it.

"Rag dollies," Flossie said. "And their clothes. And the thread to sew them with."

"That's three," Nan praised her little sister. "It's a good start."

"Boxing gloves," put in Bert.

"Kites," added Freddie.

"Hammocks," said Nan.

"Typewriter ribbons."

"Phonograph records."

"Water wings!"

For several minutes they called out. In the end Nan won the game. She had named thirty articles!

"Don't forget the radio," she reminded her twin as the packet boat docked at the Percy plantation.

Old Nebo met them with a wagon. No one else was around. Then they noticed that the work bell of Great Oaks was ringing wildly.

In the distance they could see men running and shouting. One group of them climbed aboard a moving truck and dashed off.

Suddenly the children saw smoke in the distance. It was curling up over the treetops.

"Jumping crickets!" cried Bert. "I bet the gin's on fire!"

"You're right, son," said the driver. "There's trouble ahead!"

CHAPTER XXI

NAN'S CLUE

"PLEASE take us to the fire," begged Nan.

"I don't know as I rightly should," said old Nebo. "You might get hurt."

"We won't get in the way," the girl promised, so the driver clucked to the team of mules and turned in the direction of the gin.

"I'm sure sorry for the colonel," Nebo said. "He's awful cut up about it. And I saw Mrs. Percy cryin'."

The air was beginning to get hot and was full of an odor of burning wood and oil. As the children neared the gin, they saw that the main building was ablaze, and sheds near by were catching fire.

The plantation fire force was at work trying to stem the flames. Neighbors had rushed in and formed a bucket brigade.

Freddie was beside himself with excitement. "I knew I should have brought my toy fire engine!" he shouted, jumping up and down.

Bert had picked up a bucket and joined the volunteers. Freddie suddenly sprang from the wagon and dashed through the crowd.

There is no telling where he would have gone, if he had not been stopped by a stream of water. He had run right in front of a hose!

"Freddie!" cried a voice.

Mrs. Bobbsey dashed up and hurried through the crowd, grasping her little son firmly by the arm.

It was a long time before the flames could be brought under control. At last a group of weary, smoke-blackened men drew aside to view the wreckage. Nothing was left but a shed or two, now empty, which had been used for storing cotton.

The sadness that settled over Great Oaks that night lifted a little in the morning. Colonel Percy, doing his best to seem cheerful, said that the gin was old, anyway, and that now they would have a chance to build a new one with more up-to-date machinery.

"It will be fireproof, too," he added. "In the meantime I'll have to use a very old one on the plantation. I'm going to look it over now."

He invited Nan and Bert to go with him on the inspection. The twins accepted readily.

"The gin is on the old back road where Mr. Hopper's trailer was parked the night of the theft," the colonel said as they drove toward the building.

There was nothing much to be seen along the road. Rain and wind had long since erased tire tracks or footprints which might have been made by the man. All they could see were hoof marks of mules and deep ruts cut by the plantation wagons.

The old gin had not been used for so long that vines had grown over the roof. The main door sagged and was partly open.

"The place needs a good cleaning," said the colonel, stepping inside. "Hello—what's this?"

"Is something the matter, sir?" asked Bert.

"I should say a good deal. If I remember correctly," replied the plantation owner, "there were several barrels and boxes in that corner. They are no longer here."

"Didn't someone on the plantation move them?" asked Bert.

"No, I'm sure none of the workers did. Humph, here are some nails, a hammer and an old cap which do not belong here."

"Could it have been the thief who stole your silver and other heirlooms?" mused Bert.

"It could have been," said the man. "We know now that he had boxes and barrels in the trailer."

"Let's look around for other clues," suggested Bert.

He and his sister searched the old gin very thoroughly. Just when they were about to give up, Nan cried out:

"Here's a man's handkerchief. It has the initial 'J' in one corner."

"And here's a card of a firm in New York. The place sells antiques!" said Bert, handing the address to Colonel Percy.

"I believe I should turn these over to the sheriff at once," the plantation owner decided.

That very night the police officer came to Great Oaks. He was greatly interested in what the twins and Colonel Percy had to tell him.

"The initial 'J' will spot the thief, and no doubt we'll find some more of the stolen silver at this antique shop," he declared.

After he had gone, Daddy Bobbsey stated that he and his family would have to leave Great Oaks very soon.

"Have you finished all your work down here?" asked Bert.

"Just about, son. I've bought not only all the fine old matching boards I need, but some splendid new lumber as well."

Colonel Percy and his wife begged them not to be in any hurry to go. As the twins were having such a good time, Mr. Bobbsey finally agreed to put off his departure for two days.

"That will give you time to return the radio," he told Bert.

Susan offered to drive him, and as many of the other children as cared to go along, to Aunt Emma's cabin the next day.

"We all want to see Aunt Emma and Uncle Eben again before we go back to Lakeport," said Nan.

Early the next afternoon Susan got out the car and they went to the sharecropper's place. Aunt Emma and Uncle Eben greeted them with genuine joy.

"I'm sure glad to get back my talking-box," the old woman declared.

This time the radio did all that was expected of it. They tuned in various programs which had a clear, full tone that delighted the elderly couple.

"I'm specially glad you came today," said Aunt Emma after a while. "We've got news for you."

"About Rasty?" asked Nan eagerly.

"That's right. My Eben's been asking some questions around. He's heard that Rasty is hiding out in a cabin across the river."

"Say, that's swell! Is there any way we can get to the place, Uncle Eben?" inquired Bert excitedly.

"Right now, you mean, boy?" asked the old man, scratching his head. "My boat's down by the dock. I guess we could get over easy enough."

"Come on, let's go!" cried Bert, already half out the door. "We must catch Rasty!"

Uncle Eben's rowboat was tied to a small dock not far from the cabin. A few minutes later they were on the river. Uncle Eben rowed in silence for a while, then he said:

"What Rasty needs is someone to look after him."

Bert had heard that the old man was like a father to some of his people. He started to ask Uncle Eben how he could make someone like Rasty behave when the Bobbsey boy noticed that they had nearly reached the far shore.

"Is there some place we can land without being seen?" Bert inquired. "I think it would be a good idea if we could get to Rasty before he sees us."

Uncle Eben agreed. A moment later the old man ran his boat into a little cove. Here the low-branched trees protected them from prying eyes ashore.

After fastening the craft, the two made their way cautiously through the woods. They had not gone far when they heard the sound of someone chopping wood. Uncle Eben, who was in the lead, stopped short. Bert suddenly pointed to a clearing.

"There he is," he whispered. "There's Rasty!"

CHAPTER XXII

A CONFESSION

A SMALL, tumble-down shack stood in the clearing. Near it, chopping away at a pile of kindling, was the young man whom the children had seen run away from Great Oaks.

"That's the one! That's Rasty, all right," whispered Bert excitedly.

"Well, what are you goin' to do now? Are you goin' to capture him?" Uncle Eben wanted to know.

Bert hesitated. "Maybe we'd better go back and tell the sheriff," he said.

"And let that no 'count boy get away again? I should say not!" returned Uncle Eben.

"All right, but we'll have to take him by surprise, I guess."

They drew off a little and talked the matter over. It was decided, finally, that Uncle Eben was to circle around and get in back of Rasty. Bert was to walk boldly into the clearing and talk to the young man with the axe. At the same moment Uncle Eben would pop from the bushes and grab the fellow who they suspected had helped the trailer thief.

"I'll give you a little head start," said Bert. "Be sure you don't let him get away," he warned.

"Don't you worry," boasted the old man. "When Uncle Eben catches somebody, they stay caught."

There followed a few moments of breathless waiting for the Bobbsey boy. He crouched among the bushes, his eyes on the clearing. Rasty was still busy at the chopping block, but he swung the axe slowly.

Every now and then Rasty would pause and look about him. During one of these times, Bert drew a long breath and walked boldly into the clearing.

"Hello!" he said. "Your name's Rasty, isn't it?"

"How come you know that!" exclaimed the woodchopper.

He dropped the axe and stared at Bert. His eyes rolled in terror as he looked around him. He was about to make a dash for the woods when Uncle Eben stepped out and grabbed the frightened young man by the collar of his shirt.

"No use to struggle, Rasty. We got you now," said the old man.

But Rasty was not so sure of that. With a sudden movement, he wrenched himself free and ran toward the shack.

Bert had been prepared for this. The lad

made a flying tackle that caught the youth about the knees and brought him to the ground. Between them they soon had Rasty subdued.

"I didn't do nothin'," quavered the frightened fellow. "You can't hold me!"

Bert planted himself in front of the quaking Rasty and looked him squarely in the eye. "You stole silver and other valuables from Colonel Percy. Then when you thought you were going to be found out, you ran away and hid. That's right, isn't it?"

The young fellow made no reply, so Uncle Eben gave him a gentle shake.

"You better tell the truth, boy," he advised. "We're going to turn you over to the sheriff, anyway."

"If you tell us what happened, maybe we'll put in a good word for you," Bert added.

This half-promise seemed to appeal to Rasty. He remained silent a few moments, apparently deep in thought. Finally he said glumly:

"Well, if I've got to, I've got to. But I didn't mean to steal nothin' from the colonel. I was put up to it."

"You mean you took the things to give to someone else?" asked Bert.

"That's right. I was workin' in the garden along the road one day when a stranger came by. He seemed like a nice man. He said he was collectin' old things for poor people and couldn't I find a few that the colonel didn't need?"

"Do you remember what the stranger looked like?" Bert asked eagerly. "Would you know him if you should see him again?"

"Reckon I'm never goin' to forget that man," said Rasty with bitterness. "After what he did to get me in all this trouble!"

"Go on," said Bert. "You took some things from the house while you were working inside."

"I didn't mean any harm," pleaded the wretched Rasty. "Seemed like the colonel didn't miss what little I took, to begin with."

"To begin with!" Bert repeated. "Do you mean you stole from Colonel Percy for some time before anything was missed?"

Rasty nodded miserably. He went on to tell how these small articles did not satisfy the stranger. Finally the man had given him a list of the things he wanted.

"I knew then he was a thief," the young man said. "But he told me if I didn't do what he said, he'd have the sheriff arrest me!"

"So you stole the silver from Colonel Percy and hid it in the wheelbarrow," added Bert.

"How do you know that?" Rasty asked sharply.

"I found a paper stuck in a crack with a list of the lost things on it," Bert explained.

"I guess you know everything," replied Rasty. Suddenly, looking up at the sky, he added, "There's going t'be a bad storm."

Bert was not to be put off this way. "You had the stolen things hidden in the wheelbarrow," he persisted. "After dark that night you went to meet the stranger. Is that right?"

"That's right, but it beats me how you know it!" said Rasty.

"When you met the stranger with your wheelbarrow, what happened?"

"There isn't much more," said Rasty. "He had a sort of truck with windows and doors in it fixed to his own car. He shoved all the Percy things inside and drove off."

Bert was overjoyed to find that the detective work he and Nan had done had been along the right track. The "truck with windows and doors in it" was Rasty's way of describing the trailer.

"What was the man's name?" the Bobbsey boy asked.

"I dunno," replied Rasty. "I never—" His sentence was interrupted by a flash of lighting and a sudden loud clap of thunder. "We're goin' to have a storm, I told you," he said. "A real bad one."

"Never mind 'bout that," said Uncle Eben, who had not spoken before. "You know you done wrong, stealin' from folks that've been good to you. Are you sorry?"

"I never meant to steal," whined the frightened Rasty, falling to his knees. "I'm never going to do it again."

"Are you ready to go back to the sheriff and tell the truth?" asked Uncle Eben. " 'Cause if you do, maybe the colonel won't be so hard on you."

With tears streaming down his face, Rasty promised, As he spoke, another flash of lightning tore the sky. The thunder that followed was terrific. In a moment the rain came down in a torrent.

"Jumping crickets! I don't believe we ever had rain as bad as this up North," said Bert, as the three hurried through the woods toward the rowboat.

The storm had become so furious by the time they reached the riverbank that Uncle Eben drew the Bobbsey boy and Rasty into a small shack to wait until the worst was over. The rain came in solid sheets, so hard they could not see across the river. It drove against the windows of the little building with such force that it seemed every moment as if they must break.

The wind rose to a howling gale. Streaks of lightning came one right after the other, followed by violent claps of thunder which made Bert jump. Both Rasty and Uncle Eben grew more and more uneasy. The sharecropper prowled about the cabin ceaselessly, and made frequent trips to the door to stare out at the river. Suddenly there was an ear-splitting crash, followed by the sound of tearing branches.

"Reckon that struck close by!" cried Rasty.

A few minutes later Uncle Eben groaned loudly. "The river's risin' fast," he said. "I'm afraid the storm has burst the dam and all the water is coming down here in a flood. Now we can't get home!"

CHAPTER XXIII

THE FLOOD

WHILE these exciting things were taking place, the rest of the Bobbsey children and Susan Percy were having their own troubles on the other side of the river. For a short while all had gone well and they had enjoyed themselves looking at Aunt Emma's handmade work.

"I'd like to send a present to Dinah," the old woman said. "This white knitted scarf ought to be useful."

Freddie, who was standing by the door, called out, "Gee, it's getting dark. It's going to rain!"

"I must shut the windows of the car. It will be flooded," said Susan, starting for the door.

"No, let me," begged Freddie. "I can run faster. And, anyway, it won't matter if I get wet."

He was out of the house and skipping down the front steps before anyone could stop him. He got to the automobile and closed the windows all right, but getting back to the cabin was another matter.

The wind by this time was blowing a gale, and the little boy could make no headway against it.

"This is a terrible storm!" said Nan inside the house as a bright flash of lightning was followed by a loud clap of thunder. "I wish Bert and Uncle Eben would come back. And where is Freddie?"

She went to the porch and saw what had happened to him. Just then came a blinding flash and a deafening roar. The girl dashed down the steps and ran toward her small brother.

"The river's—awful high," he gasped. "The water's coming up—over the bank."

This news alarmed Susan very much when she heard it. She whispered to Aunt Emma that maybe they ought to start for Great Oaks at once.

"Only I don't know what to do about Bert," she said.

Aunt Emma replied that Eben would take care of the boy, but she begged the young woman not to try driving.

"If the water gets any higher, the road will be flooded. You'd all better stay here."

Freddie was fascinated by the storm and stood with his face pressed to the window. But Flossie was frightened.

"Don't worry," Susan said. "We'll get back to Great Oaks, all right, just as soon as the storm stops."

"But it isn't going to stop. It's getting worse and worse!" Flossie wailed.

Nan was very upset when she thought of Bert and Uncle Eben. Were they out on the river in the rowboat? Aunt Emma assured the girl that the old man would not have tried to cross the stream in such a storm.

"Now you stop worrying," said the kindly old woman. "We'll just turn on this new music box and hear something nice."

Nan turned the dials of the radio, but could find no clear program. There was a good deal of crackling, but suddenly a voice came through.

"Attention, all you people below Bolltown who live near the river!" it said. "Leave your homes at once! Go to places of safety. The dam has burst! It is too late for those between Bolltown and the dam to leave!"

Susan and Aunt Emma stared at each other, their faces going white. They and the three Bobbsey children were caught between Bolltown and the dam!

Freddie turned from the window, shouting, "The water's coming up into the field! It's covering everything!"

"Get up to the roof! Every last one of you, get up to the roof!" cried Aunt Emma. "Take that coil of rope on the chair, Miss Susan," she added. "Can't tell but it may come in handy."

The young woman rushed to the porch. Already water was up to the door sill. Quickly she climbed to the railing and pulled herself to the edge of the roof. Then she helped the others up.

Fortunately the roof was not very steep. It sloped gently to the gutters and offered a fairly good foothold, even though the rain had made it slippery.

"Hurry up, now!" urged Aunt Emma.

The children needed no urging. Pushed upward by Nan and Susan, the little twins climbed toward the brick chimney. Once Flossie was nearly blown from the roof by the awful wind!

Freddie caught hold of the bricks first, then Flossie. Susan, with Nan to steady her, passed the rope around the chimney and under the arms of the little twins, binding them securely.

"There!" she gasped. "We'll be safe now, if we can just hang on until the flood goes down. Aunt Emma, are you all right?"

"Don't worry about me, honey. I'm just fine," returned the aged woman bravely.

She, Susan, and Nan sat astride the ridgepole. In a few moments they began to notice the sights around them. The flood waters, rising with terrible swiftness, had overflowed all the woods and fields about the cabin. The narrow river was now very wide, and was carrying away all sorts of things in its torrent.

First they saw a chicken coop. Then came a door, torn from its hinges and sailing along like a raft.

"I wonder where Bert is," yelled Nan to Susan above the wind. "I don't see him anywhere. Do you suppose—"

Suddenly she and the others felt the cottage under them groan and quiver. Then it tilted crazily.

"Great heavens, we're goin' to be swept away ourselves!" moaned Aunt Emma.

The next moment the cabin was torn loose and borne away on the swollen stream.

In the meantime, at Great Oaks, Mr. and Mrs. Bobbsey and Colonel and Mrs. Percy were growing more and more uneasy about the twins and Susan. As the rain and wind grew worse, and their children did not return, they became alarmed. Finally, when they heard on the radio that the dam had burst, the mothers were in a state of panic.

"We must go to their aid! They may be in great danger!" cried Mrs. Bobbsey.

"I know, but what are we to do?" returned Cousin Martha. "We are cut off from them by the flood! The roads are entirely under water."

Colonel Percy, who had been at the telephone, now came back. "I've made arrangements," he said. "We are to take the sheriff's motorboat up the river."

As the four of them started out, they noticed that the storm was slackening somewhat. By the time they reached the river, the rain had stopped and the sun was trying to shine.

"It will be a good many hours before this water is calm again," said Colonel Percy as they started upstream.

It was not easy for him to guide the motorboat. Wreckage of all sorts was strewn over the surface of the river and he had to swerve and dodge continually to avoid it.

People were afloat on the torrent, also. Some were in boats half-full of water, others clung to rafts which had once been parts of houses or barns. At one time they saw a little Negro boy astride a mule. The animal was swimming strongly without the slightest intention of giving up!

"Oh, there they are!" cried Daddy Bobbsey suddenly. "There are the children!"

Atop the runaway cottage sat the little twins and Nan, Susan Percy and Aunt Emma.

"But where's Bert?" exclaimed the boy's mother fearfully.

As the motorboat came alongside the "houseboat," the two families shouted back and forth. No one knew anything about Bert and Uncle Eben.

"I'm sure they're safe, though," called Aunt Emma encouragingly. "Eben's used to the tricks of this old river!"

How to rescue those on the roof became a problem. Already the rushing waters had carried the cabin past them. It was sweeping rapidly downstream, tilted at a crazy angle.

"We must hurry!" urged Mr. Bobbsey. "They may hit something at any moment and be flung into the muddy water!"

Colonel Percy turned the motorboat and started swiftly after them.

CHAPTER XXIV

THE COLONEL'S KINDNESS

IT was easy enough to overtake the floating cottage. The hard part was to remove the refugees from the roof to the motorboat. Twice Colonel Percy steered his craft to within touching distance of the cabin, only to sheer off sharply to avoid a collision.

"We'll never do it! We can't come close enough to rescue them!" cried Mrs. Percy despairingly.

Nan had been looking toward the shore line. Suddenly, from her high perch, she noticed that they were coming to a little cove. A thought came to the girl. She made a megaphone of her hands and shouted:

"The river's quieter over that way." She pointed. "Could you push us in there?"

"Good idea! We'll try!" her father called.

He picked up two oars in the bottom of the boat. He used one, while Mother Bobbsey and Mrs. Percy held the other. As Colonel Percy steered carefully, they slowly but firmly shoved the cabin into the cove. Closer and closer the "houseboat" floated toward solid ground. Finally it came to rest in the mud at the shore.

By this time the flood waters had drained off this section. Just beyond the cabin the bent-over plants of a cotton field had begun to dry out. Down onto these the Bobbsey children, Susan, and Aunt Emma crawled.

"I suppose my furniture is ruined," said the old woman sadly.

"Maybe not," replied Susan. "We'll take it out into the sunshine and let it dry."

While she and the twins helped Aunt Emma carry out the things, and their mothers spread them in the warm sunshine, Mr. Bobbsey and Colonel Percy went to look for Bert and Uncle Eben. It was a long search, but at last they found them, and also Rasty.

The three were sitting on top of Susan's car! The automobile had been moved by the flood and had come to anchor among the branches of a stout old tree. Eben had rowed across the stream as soon as it had seemed safe to do so, only to find his home gone. Not knowing what to do, he had picked a stationary object to stay on!

"Where's Nan?" cried Bert. "And Freddie, and Flossie?"

"They're safe," his father said.

"Is Emma with them?" asked Uncle Eben, a tremble in his voice.

"Yes, your wife is all right," Colonel Percy answered. "But your cabin is a couple of miles down the river."

Bert and the old man got into the motorboat, but Rasty held back.

"Colonel Percy, please don't put me in jail," he pleaded. "I never meant to steal your things. That wicked man made me do it."

Brokenly he told his story, and Uncle Eben added that Rasty had got nothing out of it all.

"Please let me go this time, Colonel," begged Rasty. "You'll never regret it!"

"I hope not," said the plantation owner gravely. He hesitated and then turned to Uncle Eben. "Do you think you could keep this fellow in hand, if I should turn him over to you?" he asked. "Remember, I'll hold you responsible for his good behavior."

Uncle Eben looked at Rasty, who answered quickly, "I've had my lesson. From now on I'm going to be an honest worker at Great Oaks!"

Rasty got into the motorboat. Presently the colonel picked up the others and headed for the plantation.

"I've got to find a new place to live," said Uncle Eben as they neared the Great Oaks dock.

"I've been thinking about that," said the colonel. "You and Aunt Emma have worked hard all your lives, and now I think you deserve to have things a little easier."

"We're still strong and able," spoke up the old woman. "We don't aim to let a little thing like a flood get us down."

"I am sure you do not," said the plantation owner with a smile. "What I was about to suggest is that you and Uncle Eben take the cabin on the west lane. It's empty now, and you can bring along as many of your own things as you like. There will be work in the cotton fields for you, Eben."

"Maybe you can sell some of the pretty things you make, Aunt Emma," cried Flossie, unable to keep still any longer. "You could make a lot of money!"

The old woman smiled, then she turned to the master of Great Oaks. "You sure are good to me and Eben, Colonel Percy," she said.

" 'Deed, I can't ever thank you enough, Colonel," said the old man gratefully.

The next afternoon the twins had their last ride on their ponies, then said good-bye to Topsy and Prince.

Right after breakfast the next morning the twins ran over to the plantation cabin to say good-bye to Aunt Emma and Uncle Eben.

The cabin looked very comfortable. Rasty, whistling happily, was busy cleaning the furniture which had been brought from the ruined cottage. Just as Aunt Emma handed a paper package to Nan, they heard running footsteps. Little Jimmy, the groom, came in, out of breath.

"Mister Bert, Miss Nan, and—Rasty," he said. "The sheriff wants to see you all right away!"

As the children hurried to the big house, they wondered what the police could want. Was Rasty to be arrested, after all?

CHAPTER XXV

A WELCOME RETURN

RASTY went along with the children, but he was not whistling happily now. He looked very frightened.

"I'm afraid the colonel can't help me after all," he said.

He, Bert and Nan went directly into the library of the big house. All the grown-ups were there with the sheriff and another man whom the Bobbsey Twins recognized at once.

"He's the one we saw in Lakeport. He was driving the trailer!" said Bert.

The sheriff turned to Nan. "What do you think? Is this the same man who left the Hopper trailer in front of your house?" he asked.

"Oh, yes, there can't be any doubt of it. I'd know him anywhere," said the girl decidedly.

So far no one had paid any attention to Rasty, who was trembling. Now the sheriff looked at him and smiled.

"We aren't going to do anything to you, since Colonel Percy has been kind enough to vouch for your good behavior in the future," he said.

"But we want the truth from you, mind! Now tell me, do you recognize this man?" pointing to the prisoner.

"Yes, sir, Sheriff," said Rasty. "That's the man that tempted me to steal from the colonel."

The officer sat back in his chair with a sigh of satisfaction. He looked grimly at the prisoncr.

"Well, Jackson, I guess that just about clinches the law's case against you," he said, and added to the twins, "The whole story is exactly as you guessed it. The 'J' on the handkerchief you found in the old gin was the last clue we needed to catch this man.

"It appeared that he had stolen from many other families in the neighborhood. He had used the abandoned gin at Great Oaks as a hiding place. It was far enough away from the house, so the hunting dogs never barked while he was working there.

"When Jackson found the Hopper family was away, he took their trailer," went on the sheriff. "He knew they would not report its loss for some time, so he had a chance to drive it up North."

"And sell the stolen silver!" cried Bert.

"Exactly! Jackson might not have been caught," added the sheriff, with a twinkle in his eye, "if he hadn't had the Bobbsey Twins on his trail!"

The officer told Colonel Percy that most of the valuables had been recovered at the shop whose address appeared on the card which Bert had found in the old gin. Then the sheriff went away with his prisoner, and the Bobbseys prepared to leave Great Oaks.

"I've had the very best time I ever had in my whole life!" declared Flossie.

Her whole family was inclined to agree with her. Those on the plantation were sorry to see them go. A few of the Negro workers had gathered, and as the car started down the driveway, they broke into one of the crooning plantation songs. The last the children saw of Great Oaks was this singing group, with Colonel and Mrs. Percy, Susan, and Mammy 'Liza waving to them from the beautiful, white-pillared veranda.

"It was so wonderful there," said Nan, when the place no longer could be seen.

"I'm glad the mystery of the trailer and the heirlooms was solved before we left," added Bert.

Mr. Bobbsey made only one call on the way home. That was at the Racher farm. He would not let the children get out of the car, but Tinky and his parents came to talk to them.

"Everything's a-goin' fine here," said Mr. Racher. "I got the new machinery and your lumber'll be out o' the woods in no time now."

"Pa let me get the new curtains," grinned the farmer's wife.

Tinky was delighted to learn that the thief, Jackson, had been caught, and that the boy's information had helped to catch him.

The trip home was pleasant, but not full of

adventures like the one down to the Land of Cotton. At last came the day when they reached Lakeport. Now they were turning into their own street! With a flourish and a tooting of the horn, Daddy Bobbsey drew up before their own house.

Dinah came to the doorway, hastily drying her hands on her apron. And what was this small object that dashed from the house and flung itself on the children as they got out of the car?

It couldn't be—but, yes, it was, it was!—their own dear Waggo, acting a little crazy and dashing around in wild circles of delight! Waggo, jumping into the arms of each of the twins in turn and being hugged until it was a wonder there was anything left of him! Waggo, with the same silly, yapping bark and the same love for them all in his soft eyes.

It seemed too good to be true. The twins demanded to know of Dinah when and how Waggo had returned. She said that the little dog had come home of his own accord two days before.

"He must have broken away from the person who was holding him," she said. "And was he glad to get home! I thought he'd wag his tail right off!"

Dinah went on to explain that she had mailed the entry blank for the pet show, just as Bert had told her to.

"A letter came for you this morning," she

added. "I think it is from someone connected with the pet show."

Bert tore open the envelope and read swiftly. "Why, this says Waggo already had been entered in the show—before they got our entry blank! What do you make of that, Dad?" asked Bert.

"I think there's been some mix-up, son. Why don't you call up the head of the show committee and ask him to explain?"

Bert said he was going to get at the bottom of the mystery right away. A few minutes later he came away from the telephone, fighting mad.

"I'm going to see Danny Rugg," was all he would say when his family tried to question him.

Straight to Danny Rugg's house the Bobbsey boy marched. This time the bully had no warning of his approach. He was bouncing a ball against the side of his garage when Bert came upon him.

"So it was *you,"* the lad said, "who stole Waggo and held him for ransom!"

"Aw, I didn't mean any harm," said Danny uneasily. "The ransom note was just a joke."

"Sure, and I suppose it was a joke, too, when you entered Waggo in the pet show, making believe you were his owner!" Bert said.

"Well, I was going to give him back as soon as the show was over. Anyway," added Danny, "what are you going to do about it?"

"Just this!" said Bert, and hit the bullv a

blow that made him sit down rather unexpectedly.

Instantly Danny got up and raced into his house. In disgust Bert turned toward home.

At the Bobbsey place things had been happening, too. The little twins had chattered like magpies as they tried to tell Dinah, Sam, Waggo and Snap, and the dogs, all that had happened in the Land of Cotton. Nan had just given the cook the scarf from her Aunt Emma when Mother Bobbsey happened to look out of a window.

"Here come your little friends. Better hurry, children, and bring the presents you bought for them," she said.

As they ran upstairs, Flossie said, "I s'pose they'll want to hear all about our trip. I feel sorry for anyone who hasn't been to the Land of Cotton—it's so much fun there."

Somehow or other the Bobbsey Twins always seemed to have fun and adventure, no matter what they did or where they went. Very shortly they would enjoy themselves in a different way, and the story is to be known as "The Bobbsey Twins in Echo Valley."

"Maybe we can go back to Great Oaks some time," replied Nan as she opened her suitcase and took out the box of molasses candy for Nellie Parks.

As they started downstairs, the twins could hear their little fox terrier barking a welcome to the members of the Find Waggo Club.

THE BOBBSEY TWINS BOOKS

By Laura Lee Hope

The Bobbsey Twins of Lakeport
Adventure in the Country
The Secret at the Seashore
Mystery at School
And the Mystery at Snow Lodge
On a Houseboat
Big Adventure at Home
Search in the Great City
On Blueberry Island
And the County Fair Mystery
Camping Out
Wonderful Winter Secret
And the Circus Surprise
Solve a Mystery
In the Land of Cotton
At Mystery Mansion
In Tulip Land
In Rainbow Valley
Own Little Railroad
At Whitesail Harbor
And the Horseshoe Riddle
At Big Bear Pond
On a Bicycle Trip
Own Little Ferryboat
At Pilgrim Rock
Forest Adventure
At London Tower
In the Mystery Cave
In Volcano Land
The Goldfish Mystery
And the Big River Mystery